STOP ME IF YOU'VE HEARD THIS ONE BEFORE

stories by
BRANDON GETZ

Six Gallery Press

Excerpts from Ziggy's notebook in "The Original Buffalo Man" are taken from *Short Works* by Victor E. Navarro, Jr. (Six Gallery Press, 2011).

The epigraph to "Ghosts of Buenos Aires" is taken from "The South" by Jorge Luis Borges, originally published as "El Sur" in *La Nación* in 1953. The translation used here is by Andrew Hurley, from Borges' *Collected Fictions* (Viking Press, 1998).

For Jack

FY

Table of Contents

STOP ME IF YOU'VE HEARD THIS ONE BEFORE

What Is There To Say

HER FATHER STANDS AT THE KITCHEN SINK, one long hand holding the wet wound on the back of his head. In the other is a serrated knife. His gray hair is blood-soaked, and there is a dark stain growing on his shirt collar. She asks her father about the wound. She asks him about the knife.

Without turning around, he says, It kept scratching around in there. He says, What else was I supposed to do?

In the sink, slick with blood like a deformed new-born, is her father's homunculus. It steadies itself against a used coffee mug. It's a rough-hewn thing, the idea of a man, not even tall enough to touch the faucet. It blinks flat, white eyes, and asks for a towel.

What is that? she asks her father.

I don't know, he answers. His shoulders rise and fall as he wheezes. There is blood on the tubing around her father's ears, the tubing that pumps oxygen into his old nose.

He has one hand on the handle of the tank, as always, its one wheel loose and creaky. He tells her he'll fix it, but he doesn't. She thinks he likes the way it annoys her, announcing his presence like a squeaking herald. She can't forget that he's still there, in the house he owns, alive.

The homunculus wipes itself off with the dish sponge. Under the blood, its skin is a dull gray. Its stomach, flat and rubbery, lacks the divot of a belly button. There's nothing between its thighs but a Ken doll's smoothness.

The sponge is wedged into the coffee cup, its yellow surface now a heavy red.

When it is clean, the homunculus asks to be called Blair, her father's middle name.

It climbs out of the sink. She says they should go to the ER. Her father might need stitches.

I don't need stitches, he says. Get me a band-aid, he tells her. I'll be in the garage.

The wheel on the tank squeaks. The door to the garage opens and shuts.

Blair says, It will be okay.

She doesn't know what that means.

Her father is in the garage building his machine. His round, heavy goggles make him look like some insect, some inhuman thing. Each time she steps inside, to ask him if he needs anything, he is hard at work. Dials and switches bloom from the dashboard. The pedals look stolen from a piano. Sparks fly.

Blair follows him. It holds bolts and washers, handing them to her father as he works. He's accepted the homunculus as he accepted the tank of oxygen or the mass of black cells in his lung: as if they had always been there. As if that were the natural order of things.

She watches the small thing drag a hammer across the concrete floor. She could step on it. She could crush it with the hammer. One little tap.

She wonders if it's alive.

His back to her, the wound on her father's skull is taped over with gauze. He scratches at it when he thinks she's not looking.

Where are you going? he says. He doesn't turn to look at her. He never does.

Work, she says. Then I have a thing.

Do what you want, he says. By the time you get back, I'll probably be dead.

Why *homunculus*? The word sprang into her mind when she saw it. She thought she remembered Greek sketches of a figure bent like Atlas inside the skull of a man, but where she'd seen them, or if they were simply something she'd dreamed, she didn't know.

Internet searches offer articles for alchemy and

animalcules, for *Faust* and *Frankenstein*. She finds an article on "homunculus theory of the mind," the theory of Cartesian Theater. The notion that a smaller self sits inside the brain, watching life play out through your eyes like a movie.

The problem, says the article, is how the homunculus itself would see and think. If the mind needs a homunculus to work, then the homunculus mind requires another homunculus. A smaller Blair inside of Blair, and so on: an infinity of Blairs. Blairs all the way down.

She scratches the back of her own head.

Would hers ask to be called Ronée, she wonders. Would it have hard lumps of breast, would it be as bald and blank as her father's.

The turntable gathers dust on a shelf near her father's workspace.

Under a tarp, the size of a refrigerator, is her father's machine. She wants to look, but she knows he would notice the displaced tarp. His face turns ugly when he shouts, even uglier than when she was young and he was full of life and anger. His eyes now swim with cataracts, and his mustache, once a heavy black handlebar, is ragged and white under the tubes in his nose.

She wipes dust from the top of the turntable. On the shelves beside it are whiskey boxes, each full of LPs, labeled and organized by artist: Baker, Beiderbecke, Brubeck. She finds the box marked F-H and flips through the Gs—a dozen or more Stan Getz, in cloudy dust jackets, the cardboard packaging splitting along the seams. She remembers her father introducing himself when he was younger, when he still played. G-e-t-z, he would say with a smile. Like Stan.

Carefully, she pulls one from its sleeve and places it on the turntable. On the shelf below is an old stereo receiver, and she switches it on. An orange light glows behind the tuner. She turns the volume low and drops the needle onto the record. From the two wood-paneled speakers, tucked away in the rafters, the saxophones of Getz and Mulligan begin their duel, drums and string bass skipping lightly behind them. She taps her foot to the music. She remembers her father, mustache and curls still black, dressed in a suit with his shirt collar open, and she's on her grandmother's lap, or her Aunt Linda's, and her father's long, yellowed fingers climbed up and down the neck of the bass like spiders, and he looked happy, in love even, with the sound.

One remembers, says Blair from the open door. It climbs down to the floor and walks toward her, casting a small shadow. Blair says, Please keep it playing.

Don't tell him, she says. Don't tell him I was in here.

Nodding its head to the rhythm, the homunculus says, Ron loves the music. He remembers the music.

His coughing wakes her most nights. Wet hacking, followed by heavy, wheezing breaths. She listens to it for long minutes until he calls for her.

She brings him water.

You could've put some ice in this, he says. It's warm.

He says, What took you so long?

He says, Don't call the doctor, I'm fine.

He says, Give me the goddamn glass.

Above the towel rack she hangs a poster of the periodic table of elements. In her own place, before her father needed someone, she had it in her bedroom. She'd tune to a jazz station and sink into her bed, getting high and inventing new elements. She would give them names and properties and try to fit them into the puzzle of the table, its rows and columns already so full.

Her lighter flares over the neon-striped glass pipe in her fingers. She sinks into the warm water, suds bubbling around her breasts and shoulders. She stares at the elements, trying to imagine a new metal, a new noble gas. The bowl grows black and cold. She sets it next to the shrunken bar of soap. As she washes her hair, she touches the ridges of her skull with her fingertips. She feels someone watching her, from the inside. Watching a movie of the soap dish and her knees.

The homunculus is in the kitchen. It is looking at the sink.

Ron is dying, it says.

I know, she says.

One wonders, it says. When there is no Ron.

The homunculus doesn't finish. It slides from the counter, landing heavily on the tile.

That afternoon, she schedules her first CT scan. They ask her about her symptoms. She has none, she tells them. They ask if she's at risk for malignancies, if she's had any serious injuries.

My father has cancer, she tells them.

Brain cancer?

Lung.

The scans show nothing. They are black and white, and clinically bland. Her brain looks like a halved walnut. Nothing to worry about, they tell her. She asks for copies of the scans. She schedules an MRI.

She rips down the periodic table. In its place she tacks up the printouts—the dull grays of the CTs, the bright, spongy blues of the MRIs. All the doctors tell her the same thing. She's running out of hospitals, and her insurance isn't covering the extra visits. Not medically necessary.

She sits in the clawfoot tub with all of her clothes

on, smoking a lumpy joint, trying to imagine which parts of her brain hold which memories, which wrinkle makes her feel love, and loss. Which fold is now ballooning and kaleidoscopic with THC.

Her father doesn't ask about the scans. He hardly bathes anymore, except when she has to take him to the oncologist, and even then he uses a cloth at the sink. My whore's bath, he says. He laughs darkly. He smells like death.

The house echoes with the noise of the television. A thick coaxial cord snakes through the kitchen from the living room. It runs under the door to the garage. She sees blue light.

Her father is under the tarp, banging at some inner working of the machine. The TV sits on an overturned milk crate, playing an old cartoon: animated skeletons dancing in black and white to a spooky melody. The cartoon is older than her father—older, perhaps, than her grandmother. In their dance, the skeletons break themselves apart and put themselves back together, playing the instruments of their bones. Blair stands beneath the screen, transfixed. She laughs. The wheel on the oxygen tank squeaks.

You need something? her father says.

Remember this? she says. We used to watch it on Halloween.

Her father stares.

Nana helped me dress up as a skeleton one year, she says. Remember? It was just construction paper on a black leotard. I was so cold.

She watches for a spark of recognition in his eyes. He looks caught, almost embarrassed, and she worries about the cancer, imagines it like a black worm growing fat on her father's memories. He struggles to smile and says, Of course, of course. Your grandmother.

Without turning from the screen, Blair says, We remember.

The wheel squeaks. Each night, she listens as it rolls down the hall. Her father coughs. The toilet flushes, and the faucet runs. Blair's small footsteps follow her father's, both shadows passing briefly beneath her door.

Her father swings his head to face her, eyes hidden behind the round, black goggles. The torch still sparks blue, and she sees the reflection of the flame in the lenses. Blair, near her father's feet, is washed in blue light.

I said it's late, she says. I have to work in the morning.

This is my house.

I know. But it's late.

How dare you tell me what to do in my own house.

I'm not—

Her father starts coughing and almost drops the torch. He leans against the workbench, doubled over. Blair has to scurry to avoid her father's shuffling boots. The back of her father's head is healed, she notices. A thick red scar runs through the stubble of his hair.

Don't just stand there, he says. Get me some fucking water.

She gets it.

She doesn't forget ice.

In the garage, her father is sitting on an old drum stool, out of breath. The torch is off, and the oxygen tank is back on. He breathes deeply through his nose.

You got into my records, he says.

I listened to one of them.

You should ask first. You shouldn't just take things that don't belong to you.

Okay.

Help me to bed, he says.

The tarp is on the garage floor, bunched up and stained black with oil. She sees it, then: a metal box without windows, without wheels or wings or cogs. She turns the latch. The door opens.

Inside, the walls are a mess with dials and diodes, with keyboards and switches and gray television screens. A drummer's stool, its leather cushion splitting, sprouts from the floor like a black mushroom. Instead of a window, her father has welded his one gold record to the wall. Around it are photographs: one of her mother, young and smiling; one of his bandmates, onstage after a show in a haze of smoke, her father talking with his hands; so many of her she can't count, doesn't even remember some of them, when they might have been taken. She sees her hair in pigtails, her gapped smile from when she lost her front teeth. She sees herself on her father's knee, as he teaches her to play "Chopsticks" on her grandmother's piano.

This is Ron's machine, Blair says. The homunculus is behind her. She can't tell if it's angry or just stating fact. Its tone is flat. Its blank eyes offer nothing.

I'm looking at it, she says. I can look.

She says, What's the machine for?

Ron's things.

What does it do, though? What things?

It is his last thing. He won't make anything else.

Did he make you?

I can't say.

She touches the back of her skull and says, Fine. Fuck it. He's spent his life making stupid things, stupid music, stupid gadgets. I don't care if he wants to waste the last moments of his life making another stupid thing.

The homunculus says, He made you.

Things her homunculus might remember:

- Her mother's death, when she was four.
- The way her grandmother smelled, like cigarettes and sour tomatoes.
- The snap of her father's belt, the welts it made on her hands.
- Staying up too late, falling asleep on smoky couches in green rooms, men laughing around her.
- The times her father locked her outside, in the rain, for some small offense. Crawling into his car, hiding there, until he stormed out and ordered her inside.
- When her father denied her breakfast because she slept too late. When her father denied her dinner because she'd failed to take out the trash. When her father denied her water because she showered for too long.
- When, at fourteen, the drummer of her father's band raped her in the bed of his truck, taking her virginity. His thin hands, calloused, and breath like rotten meat.
- Seducing the rest of her father's bandmates, even as they protested that they had wives at home and daughters her age.
- Wishing her father would die.

• The call, from her father, telling her he was dying. How she'd cried then, gutturally, like an animal.

When she loses her job, she's not surprised. She spent most of her shifts looking into the flat chrome faces of the store's mannequins, at her own distorted reflection. She took long breaks to smoke her one-hitter in the bathroom, and then she didn't show up at all for a week straight. Envelopes, ripped open and printed with the return addresses of hospitals and clinics, are stacked high on her dresser. Some are stamped in red ink.

She doesn't tell her father about the job so she can still leave for hours at a time. He stays in the garage all day, Blair at his feet. She wonders what they say to one another, if they have conversations. Her father used to tell extravagant stories, long jokes with witty punch lines, to other musicians, all of them smoking and sucking from the same square bottle.

When he talks now, to her, it's only to give orders. They haven't had a conversation in years.

There is a cemetery nearby, a big one with stone walls and rolling hills covered in rows of old tombstones. She walks in the shade of the oaks, reads beside the small frog pond, until it's time for her shift to end. She's not sure if her father even knows what time it is, or what time she's supposed to be home, but the routine is a comfort. It feels normal.

He is in the garage, oxygen tank in the furthest corner, tubes wound around the valve. He's wearing a full metal mask which looks medieval. The torch throws sparks off the hinges of the machine. A record is playing on full volume, brass and bass shaking dust from the rafters.

What is this, she yells.

He turns, flipping up the mask. His face looks gaunt and sallow, only half alive.

What?

The record, she shouts. Who's playing?

Ellington, he says. Listen to that bass line. Wendell Marshall. Fuck, that man could walk.

She listens, tries to isolate the bass, following it note for note. The saxophone is manic and cries out for attention, but she concentrates on the bass, on the background, nodding along as the other instruments jump from solo to solo, the bass a constant, holding it all together. Her father is sitting in the machine on the small drummer's stool, mask up and eyes closed, torch dead on the floor, fingers twitching slightly on his knees as they remember the strings. Blair taps its foot nearby.

It's early morning, and he wakes up coughing. She gets him

water and he says nothing, which is a sort of thank you, or at least a kindness. He falls back to sleep, tubes outlining his hollow face, and she listens to his strained breathing. She touches his hand; it's warm but clammy. The skin is too loose from the bones, and veins rise soft and blue beneath it. Dark spots dot his knuckles.

Blair watches her from the other side of the bed.

I don't even know if you're real, she says.

One doesn't either, says the homunculus. One only knows what one senses.

I hate him, she tells it.

You don't.

You're right. But I wish I did.

Ron is sorry, it says. He can't say. That's why one is here. One can say it.

Why can't he say it?

The word died in his mouth once. He cannot revive it.

Just once, she says, I want to hear him say it. To me. And mean it.

He won't.

The next day, she finds her father on the floor of the garage. He is on his back on the oil-stained cement, a large cut bleeding above his eye. Blood smears one corner of the ma-chine. The oxygen tube has been ripped from his face, and his breathing is labored. She stands over him, watching his chest struggle up and down, and she thinks about telling him the truth—her job, the endless doctors, anything—but nothing seems important enough to say. It isn't until after the ambulance leaves that she realizes Blair isn't there.

She looks for it room by room. She says its name. The house is empty.

She takes the turntable from the garage. The stereo nearly topples as she rips the cables from its back. From a random box, she chooses a record, and she takes both to the bathroom, where her brain still papers the walls. She sets the turntable on the toilet, plugs it into the small speakers on the sink. She turns the LP over and looks at its cover.

It's an album by Gerry Mulligan's quartet. The name of the band is lettered in blue and yellow across the top, the album title in white beneath it, over a photo of the sax man posing in the dark with his instrument. On the back, there is a black-and-white picture of the four jazzmen crowding together with their instruments to read from a music stand. Here, above the track listing, the title has a question mark.

She looks at it for a long time, that simple curl of punctuation.

A question begging an answer.

Then she slips the record from its sleeve. It's old, heavy vinyl, a little dusty, a deep scratch running through the grooves of one side. She sets the record on the platter, drops the stylus, and closes the lid, and the speakers begin to crackle to life with baritone sax. She turns the knobs of the faucet, lights a pumpkin candle on the windowsill as warm water fills the tub. She ignores the sax and trumpet, listens only to the bass. Slow, methodical. Holding the whole band together. The water's off, and white suds float like glaciers over the surface.

The bass keeps thrumming, one track to the next, a heartbeat. She slips into the water until the suds are at her throat. Her eyes focus on the printouts on the wall. They stop to concentrate on one of the color-coded MRIs. There is my brain, she thinks, each layer a different blob in the same palette: purple, yellow, red, blue. She stares into the lines and ridges, searching for its spine along the ridges of the cortex, its smile somewhere near the thalamus. She's still looking when she takes her father's razor from the soap dish. The bass keeps its even pace, the trumpet traces the sketch of a melody, and she unlatches the blade from its casing. She's still looking as she presses her thumb along its edge and feels its bite. The record hits the scratch, and the sax blows the same two notes, two notes, two notes. She's still looking. With both hands, she parts the hair at the back of her head, and begins.

Stop Me If You've Heard This One Before

It starts with a chess board. Rows of pawns flicker blue like stove flames on each side. Behind them: translucent projections of inbred royalty, bucking stallions, twitchy bishops, crumbling castles. Tiny gouges and cigarette burns perforate the board's surface; brown water-damage blobs and coffee-cup rings bleed over the black and white squares. All game pieces are the same ghost blue. God and the Devil know whose pieces are whose.

God always gets first move, so he twinkles his nose Bewitched-style and a stallion on his side leaps a pawn and lands L-wise on a black square. God's got a face like a beatnik who just tripled his money in Vegas. His hair coils at the back of his head in a loose, unwashed bun, held in place with a No. 2 pencil.

"You always make that move," the Devil says. He gives God the finger, swigs vodka from a flask (carved from mammoth ivory by the first murderer), and pushes his left-most pawn two spaces. "Should've played Yahtzee," he says. "You know I love Yahtzee. They got three boxes here."

He gestures a manicured hand toward the shelf of boardgames on the café wall, where a pigtailed toddler in flowery overalls stands frozen with her tiny hands reaching for Hungry Hungry Hippos. The whole Universe is in freeze-frame while the game's in play. One twinkle of God's nose and Space/Time hits Pause, cuts out all the distractions. Even the steam from God's coffee mug hangs in the air like a projection. When he drinks, the steam stays above the table, hovering, waiting for God to set the mug in the same place. The real chess pieces—plastic, made in Taiwan—rest in a Crown Royal bag beside Sorry! on the game shelf. The Devil licks his lips and the bag bursts into blue flames that flicker like chess pieces.

"That was a waste," God says. "That bag could have held a heartbeat. It could have held a dozen strawberries or a hundred cigarette butts." As he says this, he tries to see it in metered verse on page 21 of his new chapbook. He's got a book for every year since the first Big Bang; self-published papyrus bundles tower in stacks around his library, as high as Heaven's ceiling. He tugs the pencil from his hair—the thick tresses oil down his neck and shoulders—and jots *It could have held a heartbeat or a hundred cigarette butts* on the back of his receipt. Once he gets home, he'll type a poem on a clunky Remington he stole from Ezra Pound's attic. (Reached down from a low cloud and dragged it straight out the attic window.) When he types the poem, he'll send it to the Devil, by post. They exchange infrequent letters, often with family pictures (Jesus as a toddler on the goat ride at that Sumerian theme park; Legion smiling their toothy smile and holding a virgin's head atop an Aztec pyramid; Mary Magdalene in her wedding dress), and also poems and personal anecdotes and long jokes (*God and the Devil walk into a saloon…*).

The Devil's fingernails, painted with yellow smiley faces, clack a rhythm on the tabletop. Beneath his gray pin-stripe jacket, his chest is bare and ribby and tattooed with an orgy of beautiful, big-breasted women in Mardi Gras masks. They all smile, or bare their teeth. The Devil loves this point in the game, when both he and God already know each other's moves, when the game is just a formality to finish out, like crashing a car.

God nose-twitches a pawn one space forward. "We should have done this at a public house. A saloon, or cantina."

"A saloon?" the Devil says. "Take this, if you want a drink." He offers the flask.

God takes a gulp of his coffee, steam static above the table, then says, "I don't mean for booze. I like the neon signs. I like the cigarette and brimstone smell of all those stale prayers. Then it feels like we're playing a game, like something hangs in the balance. Here, these people are just lonely bank tellers and high-school masturbators and teenage girls posting vampire poetry on Instagram. No wonder you insist on coming here."

"Who doesn't enjoy the company of masturbators?" the Devil says. "Anyway, I like how the mugs all match, even down to the nicks in the handles. Besides, my house is full of cigarette smoke. Smoke everywhere." He coughs for effect and adopts an Appalachian accent: "I gots the black lung, Paw!" He thinks it would be funny to push over all the frozen people or to draw penises on their foreheads or to put his penis in their mouths. They look so stupid, with latte foam on their lips and cell phones in their hands. He looks at the toddler and hopes she'll grow up to kill her husband or drown her children. He blows her a kiss, but God snatches it out of the air and rubs it on his jeans.

"Stop kissing," God says. "We're playing a game here."

"Yeah, but where are the souls?" says the Devil. "You know I wanted to play high-stakes. Remember the poker we played over Job? Most fun I've had since the Fall."

The Devil's fingernails sneer, but his face keeps its sardonic smile.

God, of course, remembers the poker they played over Job. How could he forget? God played three Kings.

The Devil dropped a flush, and a tornado sucked Job's kids through the roof of his house. After that, they switched to chess.

"I'm writing a poem," God says. "About God and the Devil. You're in it."

"Why do you keep that up?" the Devil says. "You can orchestrate the most beautiful genocides but you can't write one decent sonnet. At least get one of your precious muses to tutor you."

"I only let you read my books," says God, "because I don't care what you think."

It's a lie, and the Devil knows it. He also knows he gives the best critiques. Poetry is a devil's art.

Instead of laughing or punching God in the face, the Devil shakes his head, takes another swig of the flask. It tastes mildly of bone. He licks a stray drop from the ivory casing with a forked green tongue. God shrugs. He's used to the Devil's theatrics. They're as old as the game the two are playing. Like the time the Devil showed up to play as a giant grub. Or the time he sneezed and lit London on fire. He didn't even have a cold.

"I'm bored," the Devil says. He points to the toddler. "Let's play for her. I want her to murder somebody."

God says, "Christ. That is high stakes. She's going to be Secretary of State. One of her grandsons is going to blow up the moon." With his pencil, he writes *A mammoth's grandson smoking / In the attic of the moon* then scribbles it out.

"It's all the same to me. She'll probably fuck before marriage or leave her house during her period anyway." Then the Devil says, "Stop me if you've heard this one before. God and the Devil walk into a bar. In the bar are a priest, a rabbi, and a white Southern Baptist minister. In each holy man is a thick, veiny dildo. And in each dildo is a seed from the Tree of Knowledge. God walks up to the bar and orders a virgin daiquiri."

"I wouldn't order that," God says.

"I know," the Devil says. "It's just a joke."

Meanwhile, the knights snort restlessly on the board. The kings are trying to look up the queens' skirts. The bishops are wondering just how young the pawns are.

"Anyhow, God orders a virgin daiquiri. The Devil orders a Flaming Blue Jesus. Ever had one of those? It's 151 rum, Rumple Minze, SoCo, and tequila. They set it on fire. My favorite."

"Why do you get your favorite drink and I'm stuck with a virgin daiquiri? Couldn't I get a White Russian?"

"The joke wouldn't be as funny with a White Russian," the Devil says. "So the Devil orders this flaming shot, and the holy men are all perched uncomfortably on their barstools, with these dildos up their assholes, and the bartender says something none of them hears. The priest thinks he said something about his father and drinks a full tumbler of whiskey. The rabbi thinks he said something about his mother and downs his last half of vodka tonic. The Baptist punches the bartender in the mouth. Because, and I forgot to say this, the bartender is black. And an atheist. The Devil slams his shot glass down, leans over the bar, and says, 'I'll take another Jesus.'"

The Devil laughs so violently a leech shoots out his nose. It squirms up someone's pant leg and disappears from this story.

"Nothing funny about Baptists," God says. He has heard this one before, at least twice. He wants to get home and make the penne Bolognese he promised Jesus and family before the kids come over and wreck the cloud couch and he can't think straight. Except he wouldn't mind canceling dinner with Jesus. Kid always brings bread and fish and does that wine trick with a jug of spring water and pretends it's just as good as an aged Pinot noir. Plus, this poem is begging to be written. Pencil scratching laces across the receipt in tight, swirly lines. *God and the Devil walk into a saloon / On the Moon / And blow up a cigarette butt / In Eden's lagoon.* He draws a frowny face beside it. He hates rhyme. Across the table, the Devil's fingernail frowns too, nudging a rook from one corner.

"It's just a story. You like stories," the Devil says. "Anyway, that's just the way I heard it in this milonga club

Down South. Don't shoot the messenger."

The Devil moves a pawn diagonally six spaces. It slumps on the board, starts to whimper. God moves it back to its original square. They're both bored with the game but stay out of eons of habit. The game pieces are still almost all lined up on their respective sides.

"The problem here," the Devil begins, "is we're not playing for anything. We've lost our edge."

To punctuate this, he crushes the ivory flask in his fingers and salts the carpet with it. The bone dust piles up into a tiny, mouse-sized mastodon. It shakes its small, blunt head, lifts one stumpy foot, pats its long tusks with its trunk. The Devil squashes it with his pennyloafer. He imagines the dead mastodon is God and the spreading red stain is Hell bleeding out over the carpet of the Universe. It scares the Hell out of him. What would he do with a whole Universe? How would he manage the paperwork on a gazillion souls? Who would play him in chess?

He says, "Let's play for a romp in the clouds with that Virgin of yours. You should see how she looks at me. Like a hellcat. You win, you get a double-team with Queen Isabella and Marilyn Monroe. Fair?"

"Keep your mind out of the virgins," God says. "Focus on the game." Instead of taking his turn, he draws a kitten in the margin of his notes. A kitten, he thinks, could be a poem, if written the right way.

By now, the kings are fucking the queens doggy-style, air-high-fiving each other from across the board. The knights are leaping around like it's a barrel race instead of a chess game; one knocks down the turret of a castle. The bishops are flogging the bishop onto frightened pawns. Nobody is winning this game. Except maybe the kings.

God stands and tucks the receipt into his back pocket. "This is the part where I say the fates of souls can't be left to games," he says. "Except that's a tired game to play. We always say the same things." He takes a corduroy jacket from the back of a physics professor's chair. The sleeves are too short, but he only has to wear it for a minute. The atmosphere is too cold for just a T-shirt. He holds out an ornately hieroglyphed canopic jar, and one by one, the chess pieces jump in: the pawns run, playing tag along the way; the castles hop like tied-up hostages; the bishops tuck themselves back into their robes and slink over; the kings begrudgingly pull out and offer the queens their arms. They all burn blue together inside the jar until God closes the lid—and snuffs them out.

The Devil lights a cigar even though he doesn't like the taste. He saw a movie once in which the Devil smoked cigars, and he's been trying to take up the habit. After one puff, he grinds the burnt end into the professor's cranberry bagel. Ashes blacken the cream cheese. He takes off his jacket and hangs it on the man's chair. A blonde in a rabbit mask, tattooed near the Devil's left nipple, winks. She blows a kiss. God catches it, wipes it on his jeans.

"I still want that little girl," the Devil says.

"We're not playing for her," God says, waiting for the Devil at the door. "We're not playing for anyone. Let them have their lives. Next time, we'll play Twister at my house."

"Your house is too cold."

"A saloon, then. You bring the Twister mat."

They leave without shaking hands or kissy-kissing both cheeks. Time unsticks, and the steam from God's coffee dissipates. The toddler still can't reach Hungry Hungry Hippos. Her mother calls her and she drinks her hot chocolate. The professor takes a bite of his bagel and tastes the ashes before he sees them. He stares at the cigar butt on his plate and poeticizes its impossibility in the jargon of physics. The espresso machine whistles and the radio plays piano and women laugh and teenagers text secret prayers into telephones. The board still sits on the table, ghost-blue clumps of horse shit on its squares.

White People

THE WHITE PEOPLE MOVED IN on the second day of summer. My wife said they were albinos.

"Albinos have pink eyes," I said. "Like mice."

"Did you see their eyes? Were you up close in their eyeballs?"

I wasn't, and said so.

"Maybe theirs are dark pink. Maybe they're some other kind of albino. Australian or something."

My wife, Midge, thought everything exotic came from Australia. Ever since she bought a jar of Vegemite from the international aisle at the supermarket. She thought it was the zaniest thing. "Why don't they just use margarine?" she'd asked me, grinning. She was proud of herself for trying something exotic.

The husband—Mr. White, my wife called him— mowed his lawn in shorts and a T-shirt. Mrs. White sunbathed on a plastic lounger, big moviestar sunglasses covering her eyes. She never turned a shade darker; if anything, her skin and hair became more radiant. Midge and I would argue about this, me insisting that the wife was whiter, Midge replying that Mr. White was the brighter of the two. But when we saw them side by side, framed inside their open front door, when we took over a plate of macadamia cookies, any differences in whiteness were only a trick of the light. A certain shadow on the cheek or the elbow. The white people were simply an absence of color, from their eyebrows to their fingernails, white as a blank sheet of typing paper.

"We brought cookies," Midge said.

"Thanks," the Whites said.

"Your yard looks good," I told Mr. White. "Real green."

"Thanks," Mr. White said. "Here, let me take that plate of cookies." The Whites were both smiling. Midge and I were smiling. The sun was hot on our necks, and there were kids shouting in the street, punctuated now and then with the splat of a water balloon.

"We would invite you in," said Mrs. White, "but we're fumigating."

"Oh," said Midge. "Is it silverfish? We had a silverfish problem. They were getting into the Wheaties, even. We had to go stay at my mother's."

The Whites looked at each other. They were a good-looking couple, the white people. Symmetrical faces, slim jaw lines, and high cheek bones. Mr. White had his white hair cut short and styled in an old-fashioned way, how my father might have worn his hair in the war. Mrs. White's lipstick was white against her powdery skin. A white ribbon held back her hair, and she wore a modest little white dress. It was true, their eyes weren't pink. They were white on white: iris, pupil, and all, thin round lines distinguishing what was what. That was a little disconcerting, the colorless stare of the white people, but with contact lenses and a little rouge, they could've looked like any young couple this side of the Missouri.

"My," Midge said, looking at the wife's dress. "How do you keep your whites so white! Do you use baking soda?"

Mrs. White then looked nervous. Mr. White looked like he might drop the cookies right there on the front stoop. Leave it to Midge to say something off-putting to the new neighbors. When the Fayads moved in down the block, she'd asked Mr. Fayad when he was going to bring all of his other wives over. He'd shaken his head and told her he was from Chicago.

"Do you need someplace to stay?" I asked. I didn't want to, but in this neighborhood, you had to be polite. It was in the Neighborhood Association bylaws. Thou shalt be kind to your neighbor. "I mean, if you're fumigating?"

"Oh, no, we're fine. We're used to it." Mr. White took one of the cookies from under the Saran Wrap and began to pick at a nut with his fingernail. The beige of the cookie looked so out of place in his hand I wanted to take it away from him and give him, I don't know, a shaved coconut or something. The color didn't belong. That's when I noticed they'd whitewashed the house, from its old dusty yellow, and the walls behind them had been re-paneled in pale white beadboard. I didn't like it. I didn't like the whole scene. I wanted to take the cookies and go. I smiled a big Neighborhood Association-trained smile and said, "Midge, it's about time we started dinner. We don't want to miss Beat the Clock."

"Beat the Clock doesn't come on for an hour, darling," Midge said because Midge can't pick up a hint to save her life.

Mrs. White widened her smile and took the plate of cookies from her husband. "Yes, it's also about time we started dinner. We don't want to miss Beat the Clock." She turned into the house, white dress flouncing, and Mr. White closed the door.

Midge looked like she'd just been told her Jell-O casserole tasted like snot. Which it did. "Can you believe that, Harold?" she said. "The nerve!"

The nerve, all right. The nerve we had to interrupt the

white people. We should have minded our business. This is America. You have the right to be a white person without somebody having something to say about it. You have the right to be any damn color you please. I could still see their white eyes looking down at me like wet leather, and it gave me the willies. I knew we'd made a big mistake. Per Neighborhood Association bylaws: Thou shalt leave your neighbor in peace. Midge and I had broken that peace.

"Harold, agree with me, will you? I can't stand here all day waiting for you to agree."

"Honey," I said, "I disagree. Full stop."

She knitted up her brow like she does when I don't agree. "Harold. Those people shut their door in our faces. After I gave them cookies. That was my mother's recipe."

"Honey bear, what did you want, a ceremonial eating of the cookies? We gave them some welcome cookies, they took them, end of story. Let's go home. I'll grill something up. Some of those burgers you like, with the mayo in them."

Midge was huffing and puffing up the walkway to our front door. "*Harold.* That is *not* the proper way to accept a welcome into this neighborhood. It says so in the Neighborhood Association bylaws. Thou shalt accept a welcome with a welcome in return." Her voice was squeaking because she was trying to keep her voice down, on account of the white people being just next door. "They were *supposed* to invite us in and offer us coffee or scotch, and we were *supposed* to sit around and chat idly about how is the weather and how do they like the neighborhood, while Shores of Waikiki plays on the phonograph. Then we say, Oh, gosh look at the time, and they say, Golly, yes, time flies when you're meeting new friends, and we go home and have dinner just in time to watch goddamn Beat the Clock. That is how things are done, *Harold*. Now how will things be between us when we all show up to the neighborhood luau in August?"

She threw open our door and went straight to the bar to fix a scotch and soda. That one down, she fixed another, then a third, which she offered to me. The TV was still on, and the newsman was saying something in a stalwart tone about the Russkies. I went to the window and lowered the Venetian blinds.

"What are you doing?" Midge said.

"Subterfuge," I said. "Espionage."

"Don't talk to me like I'm a soldier, Harold."

"Yes, sir."

She rolled her eyes and walked over to where I was by the window. I stuck my fingers between two of the slats of the blinds and plucked open a space to see through. "Have a look?"

My wife smiled. If there's one thing in the whole world she loved, it was spying on our neighbors. Mrs.

White was in the kitchen, chopping something on the counter out of view. Mr. White was in the back yard hosing his azaleas. They were dripping nearly dead with water. He'd put on his wife's sunglasses for the task, and looked like some black-eyed bug man with a water-hose proboscis.

"What do you think they're fumigating?" Midge said. "They don't have a tarp up or anything. Don't you need a tarp for that? One of those colorful numbers?"

"They're not fumigating anything. Fumigating us," I said. "Getting rid of the pests."

"Speak for yourself."

"I'm speaking for the Whites. We were pestering. Did you see how nervous they got about their laundry?"

"It was a harmless question," Midge said. "Any wife would ask that. Lord knows your whites don't even count as white compared to that man's trousers. And I use lye soap."

"Hush, honey bear," I said. "She's about to throw something in the skillet."

Mrs. White threw something in the skillet. We couldn't tell what it was. It was so white we couldn't even discern the texture of it from our vantage point behind our venetian blinds.

"Did you ever see them eat before?" Midge asked.

"No," I said. "I never noticed. I figured they ate like anybody. Steaks, potatoes, and casseroles. Maybe a TV dinner if they felt lazy."

"Me either. I never watched them eat."

"It's in the Neighborhood Association bylaws. Thou shalt not watch your neighbor eat."

"No it isn't."

"Then let's keep watching," I said. "I want to know what that is."

Beat the Clock came and went. Midge and I watched the window in shifts. She toasted some Wonderbread and slathered it with Vegemite, and I fixed two more scotchands. The white just kept sizzling in the skillet, if that's what it was doing. There had been no change in its color, no discernible smoke or odor. Mrs. White was somewhere upstairs; Mr. White was reading a book in the living room. From so far away, we couldn't read the title.

"What if she doesn't have the heat on?" Midge said.

"She does," I said. "I saw her light the match."

"What if it was a trick? She knew we'd be spying so she put some cotton balls on the stove to fool us."

"That isn't cotton. It isn't anything. It's just white."

Midge had her blouse unbuttoned at the top by now, and it was hard to stay focused on the task at hand. She was gorgeous when she was a woman on a mission. She was blushing from all the scotch, and her chest was flushed pink. "It can't be nothing. Christ on an axle, it has to be burning to a crisp in there."

I looked again through the blinds. "Nope. It's just the same as it was." It was getting dark, so I turned off the lights so they couldn't see us peering through the window. Then I got the idea that maybe they'd see there were no lights on in the house and get suspicious, so I told Midge to turn on the lights upstairs, but close the curtains so nobody could see in. She did it and came back and mixed another drink. She'd taken her blouse off upstairs, and now she was just in her slip and skirt.

"It isn't neighborly," she was saying. "That was my mother's recipe. I spent two hours making those goddamn cookies, the least I could get would be a thank you and a goddamn pleased-to-meet-you and a goddamn Shores of Waikiki. What happened to our Shores of Waikiki, Harold? I loved that album."

I was only half watching the white people's kitchen. Mostly I was looking at Midge. "It was scratched, honey bear. I'll get you another."

She sniffed. "We should go on vacation. When was the last time we went to the beach?"

"Before the twins were born," meaning my brother's twins, Anna Lisa and Anna Maria, two perfect little angels. "Remember, we had to use our vacation time to see the twins."

Midge slumped in her chair. "I miss the beach," she said. "Little umbrella drinks in coconut cups. Everybody in their bikini tops and nobody gives a damn."

"We'll go to the beach," I promised. By that time, neither of us cared much about the white people. I took one last look out the window and saw that the skillet had been removed. I didn't see the Whites or the skillet anywhere; there weren't any lights on except in the kitchen.

Midge and I went to bed, and boy, did we. That was the night we conceived Doreen, our first. We had it so many ways, I'm surprised we didn't have triplets.

The next day, the Whites were still in their white house, going about their business. Mr. White was grilling on his patio when I got home from the office, and of course, the burgers were blanched straight white like somebody'd leached all the color out of the meat. But it was almost definitely hamburger, and after that, I stopped asking questions. This is America, and if you want to eat a white hamburger, that's your prerogative. That's freedom. If you went around getting suspicious of every white person doing something strange in the whole U.S. of A., you'd never have time for anything else.

The white people even came to the luau in August. They brought a mayonnaise salad. What else was in it, Lord knows—the whole thing was like milk soup. I tried a little bit, and it wasn't bad. Kind of smoky, with a hint of cayenne. At first Midge was icy, on account of the whole cookie fiasco and also because she was sick as a dog with Doreen in there gumming up the works. But me, I try to be a good neighbor. I do my best to adhere to the Neighborhood Association bylaws. I said to Mrs. White, who we'd learned by then was named Carol, "Great salad. You'll have to give my wife the recipe."

Midge frowned and continued sipping her orange juice from a little plastic coconut. There was a pink umbrella stuck in the drink, but she wasn't in her bikini, on account of Doreen, and she wasn't happy about that—she would say, looking in the mirror in our bedroom, not even wearing her slip, "What kind of summer is this. I'm as white as the neighbors." But to me she still looked like Nancy Olson in *Big Jim McLain* in her luau dress. Gorgeous.

"I'll have to give your wife the recipe," Carol said, and her husband handed her a plastic coconut full of milk.

"How do you like the neighborhood?" I said to Don, the other White. Fayad and a couple of the other neighbors were trying to get a limbo game started up across the yard, and John Burnstone, President of the Neighborhood Association, was grilling hot dogs and pineapple slices on his big gas-power barbecue. Don was cradling a heaping plate of his wife's salad, shoveling it up with a plastic spoon.

"I bet it's a lot different from Moscow," Midge said snidely. "Not as many polar bears."

Midge was alternatively convinced the Whites were

either KGB or Martians. We'd spent many a night getting half undressed by the window and staring into the Whites' but all they ever did was read books and overwater their garden and burn pale, amorphous foods they got from God knows where, certainly, Midge said, not the Food-Plus supermarket. We didn't see any clandestine radio broadcasts. No flying saucers scooting about their chimney. And as an American, I believe innocent until proven guilty. I believe, lacking hard evidence and a fair trial by the jury of one's peers, you can do as you like, even if it means absolutely murdering what were once prize-winning azaleas that some of us would've killed to have in our own back yards.

Carol looked puzzled and sipped on her coconut. Don gulped down a mouthful of salad, smiled his white teeth, and said, "It's a lot different from home." Then he laughed, a good old *ha-ha*, and gave a thumbs-up, about American as you please.

The limbo game got off the ground, and everybody in the neighborhood was lining up to a samba tune playing on John Burnstone's hi-fi, which he'd dragged out onto his patio just for this purpose, and husbands and wives in bright Hawaiian shirts indulged in their God-given right to shimmy beneath a stick held aloft at chest-level. I asked Midge if she wanted to limbo with me, limbo being one of the highlights of the annual luau, but Midge was already running to find someplace to throw up, so I asked the Whites if they were game, and they both stretched their white mouths into grins and followed me to the samba line. Some of the bystanders were cheering us on with beers in their hands, or plastic coconuts for the ladies, and the sun felt good on our skin, reaffirming then and there the reason for luaus, to come together one and all as citizens of the Neighborhood of God's Green Earth.

I sambaed up to the stick and shimmied under as best I could, bumping the bar with my chin. Fayad and McAvoy, the stick-holders, gave me a good attaboy, and we all laughed, and next up was Carol. She stepped up to the stick and stopped.

"Go on under!" I said. There were some cheers from around the yard, and Don stood behind her with that grin still on his white face. Then she began to bend backward. She kept bending till we all heard a loud crack, and the cheers, let me tell you, stopped so quick you thought you heard crickets. Carol bent back till her head was in the grass, then she walked straight under the limbo bar, all bent in half. It was summer, and the lady's dress wasn't a long one, but a set of thick white panties kept her modest. On the other side of the bar, she popped back up and smoothed out her dress. There was grass in her white curls, and she was smiling like she'd just won a million bucks. We all listened to the samba and the sizzle of pineapple on Burnstone's barbecue, and then somebody started a slow clap, and we all started clapping, especially Midge, who felt she'd just been proven right and said so later, that they had to be Martians, only a Martian could limbo like that. I wasn't so sure, because I wouldn't put it past the KGB to train a woman to snap herself in half. Or maybe the Whites had retired from the circus to become decent Americans, it wasn't any of our business anyway. That was implicit in the Neighborhood Association bylaws: Thy neighbor's circus past is none of your beeswax.

The Neighborhood Association awarded Mrs. White the First Place Pineapple in the limbo competition, and about a month later, just before the first day of autumn, the white people moved away. One night we were watching them sit on their sofa through the blinds with all our lights off, the next they simply weren't there, the whole house emptied top to bottom. Midge said they'd taken their flying saucer back to Sydney or wherever and good riddance. After that, we didn't spend so much time peeking through the blinds and making love with our socks on. Midge got big with the baby, and we went back to watching *Beat the Clock* and all our other favorites, shouting out the answer to the Jackpot Clock when we knew it.

The Original Buffalo Man

Ziggy Najanski couldn't sleep. He hadn't slept last night either. For a week, he'd been waking up with pains in his chest and little bruises on his skin like he'd been pinched by children or goblins in his nightmares. He was in his room, wide awake at some ungodly hour, heading for another double all-nighter fueled by caffeine and delusions and a pathological avoidance of anything resembling death. At some point, he'd taken a couple of pills he found in a plastic baggie, sat on the floor, and shuffled through a stack of cassette tapes until he found The Incredible String Band, the greatest band of the '60s. He could remember sitting on Japanese cushions in Georgette's apartment on Negley Avenue, a hundred sticks of incense burning, smoking grass, *The Hangman's Beautiful Daughter* playing on her hi-fi. She'd fucked him twice, that time and one other, in his car in Highland Park, in the spring of 1969. He missed her.

By now she was probably dead or married, which amount-
ed to the same thing.

He put the tape into the little boombox he'd picked
up at a yard sale in the '90s and fast-forwarded until he
got to "A Very Cellular Song." Then he turned the volume
up as loud as he dared and sat on the floor with his back
against the bed, letting the kaleidoscopic music swirl into
the room, Mike Heron singing, *Lay down, my dear sister
/ Won't you lay and take your rest / Won't you lay your head
upon your savior's breast*, bidding the world goodnight. That
trippy harpsichord and somebody buzzing on a kazoo, and
Georgette was letting him kiss her shoulder, as white as
some unspoiled moon.

He woke in the dark, the cassette player silent and
an ache in his gut. He fumbled for one of his piss jugs. A
few half-gallon milk containers were lined up near the bed
because it was a hell of a thing to walk all the way down the
hall in the middle of the night, and one of them had to be
empty enough, though he'd had a couple of overflows and
the room had held the stink for weeks. As he held up jug
after jug, weighing them in the dark, something crashed in
another corner of the room.

"Who's there?" he said. "A ghost?"

Fucking ghosts, man. Always knocking things over
when a man's trying to piss. His fingertips touched the cap,
and he started to unscrew. Another crash, this time the

scraping plastic sound of falling cassette tapes.

"Aw, come on," he called out, almost startling himself. His voice rasped like a coffee grinder, throat scarred ten times over from a lifetime of cigarettes and whatever else, but it still surprised him how much it had changed. In his college years, he'd nearly been a half decent tenor. "This is creepy," he grumbled. "You're just trying to creep me out!"

He dropped the cap, hitting over the jug as he grabbed for it. The smell filled the room, an acrid deluge that singed the nose hairs and reminded him of Crazy Bob, who used to loaf pickled in piss and carefree in the library at CMU by the Servomation food machines, hassling the girls and rapping for long hours on philosophy and aliens, unless he was in one of his crazy moods and barking whenever anybody came near. Zig crawled out of bed and stumbled through the piles of refuse, reaching for the light switch. It occurred to him he didn't remember turning the lights off. Heron had been singing, and there was that old hippie refrain, *Goodnight, goodnight*, and then he'd woken up in blackness with a bladder full of coffee. As the fluorescents flickered on, he saw a flash of movement near the hot plate. He picked up his guitar and brandished it like a battle axe.

"Come out so I can hit you with this," he whispered, begging the stygian gods of night that there was nothing to whack, or if there were, that he'd have the cojones to swing.

From behind the hot plate, sliding out of some unseen pocket of the Universe, appeared a small man. About as tall as a beer bottle, with a thick tangled beard and weaselly little eyes. He wore a blue paisley vest over a rust-colored T-shirt with an iron-on transfer of the Cheshire Cat and, in bubble letters, the catchphrase *You don't have to be crazy to live here, but it helps!* His tighty-whities were gray and stained, and he was missing one of his loafers. His exposed sock was ripped so badly all of his toes were showing. He scratched his belly button and sniffed his finger, then belched loudly.

"You know what I hate about you, Najanski?" the small man said. "You keep terrible house."

Zig blinked in the hard light of the fluorescent bulbs. The tiny man wasn't wrong: Ziggy's room was chaos of the highest order. Books stacked on top of notebooks on top of piles of hand-me-down clothes and threadbare sportcoats. Unused canvases stacked against the mini-fridge, paint-crusted slivers of cardboard stuck raggedly to loose socks. The judo book with the detailed illustrations sat butterflied on the unplugged hot plate so that he could learn the Deadly Hold to use on his friends and enemies. The hazardous line of piss jugs. And on the wall above his twin bed he'd hung several photos from years ago—the portrait of himself holding that plate of pancakes like some haggard god of breakfast, and others, too, of Aloysia and

Preacher and the crew at the video store, and some sketches Remi had done in magic marker, all taped where he slept so he could see them when he woke up. The room was a single, no toilet, no kitchen, on the second floor above the Chinese restaurant, in a building full of single rooms just like his, where nine other men just as old and lonely shared the grimy bathroom two doors down.

"Are you really a ghost?" Ziggy asked, still brandishing the guitar. He believed to his bones in the ectoplasmic mojo of specters and spooks, though he was lucid enough to know the little man could just be a hallucination. Zig had done enough acid in the '60s to break his mind and send himself rattling down the neon throat of full-blown schizophrenia, according to the docs who zapped his brain with wires and told him he'd punched a woman on the bridge near the library, calling her the Devil and swearing up and down to the good officers of the Pittsburgh PD that she was Anti-Christ incarnate, come to drown us all in the black oils of Hell itself. Hallucinations, ghosts, flashbacks—it was hard to say where the incorporeal ended and the flat-out fictitious began.

"I fucking look like a ghost? You ever see ghosts that ain't man-sized?"

Zig shrugged. "Never measured any ghosts."

"Use your eyes, Najanski. I ain't no fucking ghost, man." The small man pushed the judo book off the hot plate and scrambled onto it, sitting with his legs sprawled so black bits of pubic hair fanned out from the leg-holes of his briefs. "I'm a house spirit. Domo-fucking-voi."

"What is that, Chinese?"

"You've been huffing them eggroll fumes from downstairs too long, Zig. No, it ain't Chinese. It's old Slavic. Heinzelmännchen, hob, damavik, brownie, house djinn. Different labels for the same can of beans. Lords of the household. Spirits of the room. And your room is an atrocity for the ages. If this was still the old country, I'd have had the polevoi kill all your livestock and destroy your crops ages ago. Ain't got that kind of power these days. I can't even find my pants."

The house spirit belched again, and Zig thought the thing looked a little too much like Crazy Bob, with the beady eyes of Preacher and the ratty priest's beard of Mother the Russian, who was always shimmying into the Old Goat, the coffee shop on Liberty Avenue where Ziggy loafed. Mother, who spent half the day talking trash on Zig's paintings because he was some kind of old Russian master artiste who'd painted religious icons for churches all over the known Universe. The spirit was just a flashback, he told himself, a manifestation born of lysergic acid knocked free from his spinal cord by whatever pill he'd taken in the psychedelic ecstasy of *The Hangman's Beautiful Daughter*.

The spirit snapped its fingers. "You awake, Najanski?"

"I still have to go," Zig said, finally laying the old six string on his unmade bed. "You mind if I just use one of the jugs here?"

"You'd better," said the spirit. "The goddamned One-Armed Man's probably in the bathroom down the hall taking a shit or banging one of those toothless hookers he likes, maybe both at the same time. Guy has to learn to multi-task, only having one arm."

The One-Armed Man was the bane of Zig's existence, a vicious old war vet with prison tattoos on his neck and a thick white mustache who lived in the next room over. Once, the One-Armed Man had even thrown Zig down the stairs, and he'd laughed, the woman with him laughing too, both of them getting a good laugh that left him feeling wretched for days. He'd hunched over his coffee at the Goat, scowling at the regulars and saying mean things to Remi and Aloysia when they told him to eat something. Thinking of the girls hassling him about food made his stomach scrunch like an old mop. He hadn't eaten in three days. Food would just detonate him anyway. It made him feel heavy and had chemicals in it and who knew where those came from. He usually stuck to coffee and cigarettes.

"You draining the snake or what?" the spirit called. "I ain't got all night."

Ziggy picked up the jug he'd spilled and went to unzip. "You're not gonna watch, are you?"

"Your fossilized flesh flute? Seen it a thousand times, you giving it the old yank to that picture of the hotness on your wall." The spirit made a jack-off motion and scoffed. "'Aw, Aloysia, aw, hon, your cunt, it's so wet like the ocean.'"

Turning his back to the house spirit, Zig let loose and felt his bladder relax like a hand that's been balled into a fist for days. The stream made a satisfying sound as it thrummed against the hollow plastic. When he was done, he gave himself a shake and twisted the cap back on.

"Good old Zig," the spirit said. "Who'd worry about washing his hands when there's piss all over the floor, am I right?"

"What're you here for, just to make me feel bad? Is this like a Scrooge thing?" The bed creaked as Zig sat. "I don't like Dickens," he said. "Too many orphans. Orphans mean somebody died. You ever read Camus? Or Nietzsche? 'Underneath this reality in which we live and have our being, another and altogether different reality lies concealed.' Nietzsche said that, and Nietzsche was God, literally God."

He stared at the small, fat, vested man on his hot plate and was suddenly terrified. *You're falling down the rabbit hole,* Zig told himself. *They've shocked you for less.* Probably lock him up for the long haul in Dixmont Psych, that slaughterhouse. Not even a decent place like Hillview, where they had dances and pool tables and he and Caroline had necked all night till the orderlies caught them.

The drugs weren't as good anymore either. They'd leave you gasping like a beached fish. Somebody finds you talking to house spirits, they just shove a hose in your throat and crank the pills in till you're one breath from dead.

"You gotta get out of here," Zig told the domovoi. "I can't be talking with spirits and creatures and phantoms. I have my sanity to think about. My mental health."

"I'm pretty sure," said the spirit, "that train sailed decades ago." The spirit hopped off the hot plate and found his missing loafer under the judo book. He shoved his bare foot into it and then crouched and executed a perfect mime of the Deadly Hold. Ziggy was awestruck. Holding his judo pose, the spirit said, "First, I ain't going anywhere. I'm a house spirit, and as such I'm bound by metaphysical law yadda-yadda to this heretofore domicile. Second, mostly you can't even see me, 'cause I'm in my little spirit room drinking fern tea and carrying on philosophical conversations with cockroaches. You ever try to talk to a cockroach about Foucault?"

"Once or twice."

"Well," the spirit said, "then you know. Normally, it's a personal affront to a domestic spirit to see such a fucking pigsty, but I figured, what the hell, this guy marches to the beat of his own drum, no harm. But now look at me. You know I used to be one of the house spirits to the Romanovs? A distant third cousin twice removed, but still.

That's some shit. That's what they call *pedigree*. Somehow, four countries, an ocean, and a century later, I'm in this room with your chapped ass watching you whiz in a milk jug." The spirit did a ninja kick and sent an old notebook flying into the boombox, which landed safely on a pile of T-shirts. "Sick of it, Najanski. Sick of your face and your cock and your smells. The bylaws of the metaphysical such-and-such directly tether my physical and mental state to the condition of the residence subordinate thereof and forthwith, et cetera. Basically, your room looking like shit makes me look like shit."

Zig started mumbling an apology. The more he stared at the face of the tiny man, the less it looked like Crazy Bob. It looked familiar, though. A face he'd seen a million times, hidden and secret under that big grizzly beard.

The spirit shrugged. "Stuff the sorries, Zig, it ain't your fault. I mean, it is your fault, it's actually one hundred percent your fault, but fuck it. Thing is, I can't just run about willy-nilly. Can't even cross the threshold to the hallway. Can you imagine if I had to piss? You'd have jugs of domovoi piss stacked through the roof. But no, there's a process. A bunch of junk you gotta put in a suitcase. It's all very ritualistic and shamanistic and spiritualistic and what have you."

"I knew a guy who did some of that in the '70s. He liked to wear this robe from Brazil and say these Hoodoo prayers, then we'd all get rolling on 'ludes and get naked in Highland Park and howl at the moon."

"Getting fucked up and barking at the moon ain't shamanistic. I'm talking real Old World stuff. You know your Russian friend? That asshole you complain about always talking down to you 'cause you can't hardly paint a shape? Talk to that motherfucker. I bet he knows. I forget it all, that's how bad it's getting. Can't remember the laundry list of nonsense things. Must've been the '30s I got lugged up here. Pretty decent boarding house back then." He scratched his beard, the weasel eyes looking heavy and faraway. "Lot of fucking years in this room, Zig. Lotta years."

"You mind if I put on some tunes?"

The spirit shrugged. "Whatever you want, man. I'm gonna hit the hay. You're boring me and I'm tired of your face." His fat fingers reached out and pried open a sliver of space-time. He looked back and said, "Remember, talk to that old queen. He'll know."

Then, without so much as a pop or sizzle, the house spirit was gone. Zig slouched in bed and stared at the hot plate. He swore to himself no more pills, probably, and that he'd eat something first thing tomorrow, whatever Remi told him to eat. He didn't care if it made his stomach coil around itself like some wet snake, it'd be better than fat little hallucinations watching him piss and disrupting his dreams. He reached for the boombox and turned the cassette to Side B, sliding down onto the mattress as the room descended into the somber sounds of the "Waltz of the New Moon."

The coffee at the Old Goat wasn't anything special. Still, Ziggy hunched over his fifth cup of the day, in the corner table by the window, the coffee almost white with all the sugar and cream he'd dumped in. The Goat had been his spot for a decade, since back when you could still smoke in coffee houses and he'd held court with the punks and bums of Bloomfield, talking literature and philosophy and filling the ashtrays full of spent Benson-Hedges. In those days, Preacher was still alive and the girls behind the counter smiled at him. And they were fine ones, all of them. The Goat wasn't like that now. It was cleaner. The video store in the back of the shop had been carted out to make more room for kids to sit around with headphones in their ears. Nobody came to loaf or bum cigarettes. Most days, he sat alone.

He pulled the blue spiral notebook he kept in his sportcoat and thought he'd write something about the clean stink of the Old Goat, the air too fresh in there so you couldn't even think. Instead of writing, he marked the precise angles of random labyrinths, letting his hand trace page after page of pen-ink mazes until his thumb got a cramp and the idea of a getting stuck in a maze began to creep him out. He flipped to the next blank sheet and drew the smallest stick figure he could in the middle of the page. Beneath it he wrote, "House Spirit." A chill went down the zipper of his spine, and he drank his coffee, which was cold enough now not to hurt his teeth.

After the domovoi, he hadn't slept at all. He'd smoked cigarettes and stared at the spot behind the hot plate where it had climbed into its spirit dimension, remembering to blink only when his eyes got too dry and smoky to see. The String Band played till the cassette clicked, and he flipped it over and played it again, trying to call up again the memory of Georgette's sweet slit and fine shoulders, but each time his cock started to worm in his briefs, he saw the weasel eyes of the domovoi, those thatches of hair climbing out from the spirit's underwear, and his erection turned weird and limp and sad. As he sat in the light of his room, he couldn't shake the feeling that the spirit was watching him, that it had always been, that it wasn't a flashback or delusion but a fat little demon, a Rumpelstiltskin with a foul mouth that liked to watch him jerk off.

It wasn't long before Mother stalked up the avenue with his spastic pitbull, dog and man both wrapped in several gold-thread paisley shawls. Mother tied the mutt's leash to the bike rack and let it bark its head off while he rushed inside with all the drama he could muster, which was, admittedly, a lot. The old Russian really did look like some kind of shaman in his old-timey vest, gray wizard's beard, and layers of ornate scarves. He was a devout Orthodox, a believer of the Old Rite, who'd been painting religious icons since the age of nine and who'd done two years in a Siberian work camp for the crime of hiding church books from the Kremlin's secret police. He was also as gay as a pair of purple jeans and eyed the asses of the young punk boys of Bloomfield with wolfish fervor. The cognitive dissonance in this, he'd tell you, was an American invention. God didn't care who you fucked, and Mother could list dozens of gayer-than-thou saints as proof.

Ziggy slapped the notebook shut and mulled the words he'd use to ask for the old man's help. Mother waltzed to the counter, where Remi was reading a book on whales or Martians or something, looking as she always did, like she was keeping a giant secret from the world. Mother smirked at the young girl and said, "You wanna fuck?"—an old joke, since he often made it clear he hadn't touched a pussy with a six-foot stick since his raucous party days in Paris fifty years ago. Remi gave the Russian her customary "I'm busy" and went back to reading. Mother then turned to Zig. The dog was still barking like crazy outside. Zig could see it straining against its braided leash.

Mother nodded toward the blue notebook. "Doing something today besides being a degenerate?"

"Aw, Mother, don't start with the degenerate stuff.

I haven't slept in three days." Zig pulled his last pack of Benson-Hedges from his coat and tapped one out. He was about due for a smoke, sitting too long inside in that clean, clinical smell. In fact, he was overdue.

The Russian muttered a string of curses in Slavic. "Why don't you get a job? Why don't you do something with your miserable life?"

"I can't," Zig said, "I'm half crazy."

Mother scoffed. "Half."

"Mother, let me ask you something," Zig stuttered. "You heard of domino–domo–uh, spirits? Major domos? Domo arigato. House spirits, is what I'm talking about. Little fat guys who live in your room and look at you all the time."

The Russian narrowed his old gray eyes. "A *domovoi*," he enunciated thickly. "Where you hear about the domovoi?"

"Friend of mine," Zig said.

"Nah-nah-nah." Mother shook his head, on top of which was a flannel newsboy cap that clashed with the flamboyance of his scarves. "You're both a liar and a degenerate. You see one of these creatures? Was he wearing his boots?"

"He was wearing loafers."

"Loafers?!"—then more Slavic curses, a couple of invocations of the Virgin Mary. "Where you see he has these loafers? The domovoi, he does not wear loafers. You read about this, what, in a book?"

Zig stared into the pale surface of his coffee. Mother was staring at him with too much seriousness, it was making his skin crawl sideways and his armpits feel weird.

"You tell me," Mother said, shedding a few shawls to make himself more comfortable, "what this domovoi looked like in vyrozhdennyy loafers."

"I don't know," said Zig. "A red T-shirt, a vest like this one I had back in the CMU days. Blue paisley. The young fine ones all loved it."

A flicker of a smile twitched under the Russian's mustache. "Paisley," he muttered at the ceiling, "Madonna. Mother, your son is dying in America." The Russian settled into the chair across from Zig. "In the old country, this is what the domovoi looks like: He has a red shirt, a blue vest like the one I am wearing, linen pants, and little kamik boots. But you don't see him except when something bad is happening. He will knock on doors and walls and the spoons will fall in the night from where they hang by the stove. A barabashka—what you call it, a poltergeist. But that is just when he is angry or he is telling you death is coming."

"He knocked over my cassette tapes. He was real pissed at me."

"Neobrazovannyye svinyi," Mother spat, flecks of

mucus flying, "Of course, you are a degenerate and a bum and he does not like you. You probably don't keep your house clean. You need to sweep the dust from the corners of the house and make sure you put out tea cakes and bread by your stove, because that's where the domovoi live, under the stove."

"I don't have a stove, I can't even cook!"

"Listen to me," Mother said, very serious, wagging a gnarled finger in Zig's haggard face. "You get yourself a stove and you get yourself some tea cakes and you treat your domovoi with respect. It is very old and very rare. Someone brought that here from the old country. My mother brought one in a suitcase all the way from Vyg, and it lived in our house in Boston for thirty years."

This was it. This is what the house spirit was talking about. Suitcases. "How'd she do it, though? Some kind of Rube Goldberg trap? An evil wizard's spell? I don't want any spells around. Magic lingers."

Mother began moving his hands in the mime of a domovoi capture. "You set a suitcase beside the stove, and then you fill it with a piece of bread and dried ferns on top of a square piece of linen. When the domovoi comes to take the ferns and bread, you tie him in the piece of linen with a blue thread and shut the suitcase. And then you have your domovoi. You take it to your new house and put bread and tea under your new stove and treat him nice and he will look after your house and keep the bad things from coming in through the windows."

He had it, then. The trick. Bread, ferns, linen, blue thread, suitcase. He didn't own any of those things, wasn't even sure where to get blue thread unless one of the girls, Remi or Aloysia, had some. Did they have it the gas station? Where was a thread store? Or a fern store, even?

"You want it?" Zig said finally.

"What you mean, do I want it?" Mother's accent was always thicker when he was talking about the old country. It was the kind of accent that waxed and waned depending on context, mood, and how cute the boy was.

"Mother, I gotta get rid of it. It's creeping me out. I can't sleep. It's watching me, trying to sneak into my dreams." Zig waved his unlit cigarette like a wand. "It wants to get the heck outta Dodge. It told me so. It said it's sick."

"He's *sick*? You made the domovoi sick? Svinyi," Mother muttered. "Swine." The Russian began to wrap his shawls over the shoulders of his vest. He looked out the wide window at his forlorn mutt, now resting its head on the bare concrete. "I will do this thing. I will take your domovoi," said the Russian. "*But*—I want you to practice. You want to be an artist, or do you want to be a bum? Paint something. Write something. Play real music. If I take your domovoi, you have to make one good thing. Don't be a bum all your miserable life."

With that, Mother whisked toward the door, trailing a rainbow of colored shawls.

"What the hell was that?" Remi called from over her book.

"Aw, nothing, hon," Zig told her. "Old country stuff."

"You're not from the old country."

"Tolstoy was from the old country. He called Nietzsche stupid and abnormal. Can you believe that? Nietzsche was God, and God killed him for it."

"Whatever."

He tucked the notebook back into his coat and headed for the back door, found an empty table outside. It was morning and still cool, the sun hanging vaguely on the other side of Liberty. The colder, the better. Zig didn't like heat—he'd been born on Christmas Eve and had the cold in his bones. He stuck the cigarette between his teeth and lit it with a match. He could smell burning meat from the fancy burger joint across the street, the air hazy with its barbecue smoke. How could that be legal? It made him nauseous. He finished that cigarette and smoked another, wondering what he could paint that would satisfy the taciturn Russian, which saint he could pray to for help.

For the next week, the domovoi didn't appear. Zig stayed at the Goat from open to close, drinking as much free coffee as the girls would give him, drawing stick figures in his notebook, and smoking the rest of his packs till he had to cadge from the Narcotics Anonymous crowd that loafed at the cafe while all the bars on Liberty overflowed with Happy Hour. Mother didn't dance into the shop, or even walk by in his shawls, and Ziggy was grateful. The old Russian might've asked him about his painting progress. In his room, at night, he played tapes of old hippie rock 'n' roll and stared into the terrifying blizzard of a blank canvas. He didn't even bother to open his paints—any oils he slopped on would ruin the canvas's perfect plane. The eyes of someone were always on him, he could feel it, and even in the dead of night with the risk of the One-Armed Man in the hallway, he'd shuffle down to the bathroom to piss. He'd emptied all his jugs. He couldn't even beat off without feeling the spirit watching. When he'd nod off, finally, from boredom and exhaustion, he'd wake startled in the purple dawn and swear the mess of his room had been rearranged, but he could never be sure.

After days without a visit from the house spirit, Zig knew he had been right all along, that it had just been flashback and delusion, an acid trip revisited in the delirium of the double all-nighter he'd foolishly pulled. He shoved the blank canvas under his bed, where he couldn't even accidentally see it, then stuck a Pogues album into the boombox and tried to re-read *The Gay Science* without laughing at the title. He read the first and last pages. Shane MacGowan was drawling the lyrics to "Dirty Old Town," *Clouds a-drifting across the moon / Cats a prowling on their beat…* It was a horror movie of a song, he realized, though he'd heard it thousands of times since the days when he'd sit in the small cubicle in the aviary where he'd worked security for a while, before he'd been too paranoid to deal with the eyes of all the birds, their accusatory screams. In the song, MacGowan's sharpening an axe, threatening to cut somebody down as a train burns and sirens wail, and it was too creepy—Zig hit the stop button and sat in silence.

From the hallway, Zig could hear the shuffle of footsteps, a woman's hoarse laugh. The One-Armed Man, with one of the saggy ladies of the night who leered at him when he passed them on the way to the bathroom, wearing nothing but the One-Armed Man's stretched-out T-shirts. They'd tell him he was next, and he'd hurry away, though he had to admit it'd been too goddamn long since he'd been fucked. The last one had been Fat Diane, in '92 or '93, right there in Cheryl's apartment on that ottoman covered in cat hair, and he didn't want to remember what she looked like, or Cheryl for that matter. They'd been so high they didn't know which way was up, and that snaggletooth minx had beguiled him maddeningly. Now it had been too long, and he was sure his cock had shrunken like a salted slug from amphetamines and disuse.

"Don't get any ideas, you old prick," came the house spirit's voice. "I'm not watching that sad show tonight. Let's play cards or something."

"I thought you were gone," Zig said. "I thought you were my imagination."

The spirit lifted his hands almost cruciform. "Still here. In the flesh. Or whatever."

"Mother has the suitcase. He's bringing it. You'll be free."

The house spirit slumped on an old sportcoat on the floor. "Fuckin' A, Najanski. That's what I wanted to hear. Not as useless as you look. When's the big fat ritual?"

"I don't know. He just said he'd do it."

"Christ, Zig, you're leaving me in limbo? Sitting here in the stink of that piss you spilled? You didn't even scrub that, man. You just let it soak into the floor."

"I don't have the cleaners. The pine smell detonates me."

"Your face detonates me," said the spirit. "What happened to that song that was playing? I liked it. Morbid shit, but a nice Old World kinda vibe."

"The Russian, he says you don't come out unless you're real pissed or somebody's dying," Zig said. "Are you just pissed? I can't deal with death. Can you imagine? Being stuck in a box in the earth and you can't move? It's terrifying." Ziggy thought about that: the permanence of it, the foreverness. The black dirt swallowing his coffin like some toothless monster.

"Nobody ever dies," the spirit said. "Just slough the mortal coil and float off into the abyssal heavenly what-have-you and so forth. I know, Najanski, I seen all those secret corners. People, they just transmigrate and metamor-phosize into things you can't see. Like a cigarette, right? You got your average cigarette, it's a little white thing, your regular fucking death stick. Light it up and it burns away to just the filter, and the smoke rises out and dissipates, and you can't see it but that doesn't mean it isn't there, right? Atomized? Slipping right up into the holy cosmos."

"'Another and altogether different reality...,'" Zig whispered. He fumbled for a cigarette, wanting to test the spirit's theory, to remember.

"Ex-fucking-zactly." The spirit scratched himself and looked over at the photos on the wall. "You ain't ever gonna die, Zig. That's a fact. You'll see God and not even blink. You'll become a Son of God and a Daughter of the Revolu-tion. You're like the smoke—you'll be everywhere."

Ziggy watched the blue-gray smoke curl from his mouth and considered his immortality. It sounded plau-sible enough, and scientific, if you got down to the ele-ments of it. He imagined wafting across the rooftops of Bloomfield, sucking in the smoke of the dive bars on Lib-erty Ave, passing by the windows of the naked young fine ones as they diddled their unspoiled twats or just lounged in the altogether reading Heidegger and Hegel with The Incredible String Band playing on their stereos. As smoke, he rose higher and higher, till Pittsburgh was just a pinprick of lights in the dark below, and he was out past the white ghost moon and the neon Milky Way, in the cold black void of the whole wide-open Universe. Out that far, it wasn't any better than a hole in the ground. It was still eternity in the jet-black maze of evermore. It was still death. Smoke coiled from his cigarette, and the horror of it filled him like a heavy gas.

A knock at the door almost made him drop the cigarette on his shorts.

"You expecting somebody?" said the spirit.

Ziggy whispered back, cigarette safely between his teeth, "What if it's the One-Armed Man?"

"Then you better grab that guitar and start swinging."

"Open up, you degenerate," came Mother's muffled voice from beyond the door.

Zig unlatched the lock, and the Russian burst in, a tattered brown-leather suitcase in one hand and a five-by-seven icon of the dog-faced Saint Christopher in the other. He flopped the suitcase on the bed and set the icon carefully under Ziggy's wall of pictures, its dog eyes seeming to watch the whole room.

"Patron saint of travelers," Mother said. "He will watch over the domovoi. Now, where is the creature?"

The domovoi was gone from the sportcoat. He wasn't anywhere.

"What is this, you don't even hang up your clothes?" Mother scolded. "How do you live like this, in such filth? This is why your domovoi becomes barabashka. It does not like slovenly homes."

The Russian began to unpack the suitcase in a huff, rearranging the contents into the domovoi trap he'd described at the coffee shop. On a small linen handkerchief the old man laid a dark crust of homemade bread and a long, dry fern, along with a small wooden nail. He held a thick length of blue yarn between his fingers.

"What's the nail for?" Zig said.

"Hush, swine. That is a piece of my house, from the original frame. Eighteen-sixties, eighteen-seventies. Then he will know the smell of a clean old home and run to leave your mess."

When the trap was set, the Russian sat stone-faced on the bed. The old man stared at the wall, only moving to breathe. Ziggy sat next to him and did the same. The suitcase sat open between them, the heavy knocking of the One-Armed Man's bedframe against the wall punctuated now and then by a slap or a moan. They sat that way for years, it seemed, decades working lines into the Russian's weathered hands and face. Ziggy's cigarette burned down to the filter. He felt the ever-spinning pull of the Universe, saw his body old and lonely in the emptiness of the void. His heart pounded too loud, thump-thumping in a haggard rhythm he couldn't quite tap with his nicotine fingers.

Finally, after some thousands of years, the fern twitched. The Russian scooped the handkerchief into a ball and knotted the yarn around it, dropping it into the suitcase and slamming the lid. He triggered the brass latches, locking the case, and smoothed the worn leather with his gnarled hand. To the suitcase, he whispered, "Tishe, dedushka."

There were no sounds from the locked case, no kicks or punches or epithet-laden promises of future violence from the small house spirit.

"Well," Mother said, "that's that."

"How do you know?" Zig said. "Maybe it was just a cockroach. Or that mouse I used to feed."

"It was no mouse. I felt the soles of domovoi's shoes."

"But aren't you gonna look at it? What if it jumped out?"

"You don't look at the domovoi." The old man's gray eyes were piercing, like a couple of those murderous icicles that hung from the awning of the Old Goat in the bitter dead of winter. "To see the domovoi's face means misfortune. Domovoi is—what you call it. A harbinger. When his touch is cold…" Mother shook his head. "God save your degenerate soul."

With that, the Russian left, closing the door carefully behind him.

Zig sat on the bed and listened to the One-Armed Man's fucking till it stopped. Doors opened and closed, the toilet flushed. He looked around at the chaos of his room—the canvases and clothes, the cassettes and novels and old paint brushes. No one was watching him. The room was suddenly and fantastically empty except for himself. He sat alone in the museum of his own life, and no one was looking at what he did or did not do, no one cared to look. He could do anything, freely, beat off in every corner and piss into the wind, and he had never felt more lonely in his entire life, not even in the solitary padded cells of Dixmont. He thought of chasing down the old Russian, bartering for the suitcase back, planting the little square of linen under the hot plate to see if it would bloom into domovoi. But the spirit had wanted to leave, and Zig knew Mother wouldn't entrust the ancient house deity with him, in this room, not even with his fantastic cassette tape collection. And anyway, Ziggy wasn't wearing shoes. By the time he found his loafers, the Russian would be long gone.

Zig moved some old books from the wall near the door and, convinced the pain in his chest was only loss, sat down opposite the unmade bed and the collage of photographs. He looked at them. Remi, Aloysia, Preacher, all of them, smiling and stoic, faces from some other life, windows into Time itself, back when the Goat had been full of the people he'd loved and they'd smoked and rapped about nothing at all, because it didn't matter, the specifics, the precise arguments and litanies of philosophy and life. From his discarded jacket, he pulled the spiral notebook and flipped through the pages: small line drawings, ragged bits of poetry, maps of mazes he'd never quite finished. On the very last used page, after his stick drawing of the domovoi, someone had written *The old days had a piquant flavor / and you could count them on a ruler / they were so exact.* It was in his handwriting, but he didn't remember writing it. Not that it mattered. Lines like that were a gift from God, and he'd learned not to question their origins. At the bottom of the page, he'd also scribbled *Project: write the book to replace the Bible.*

Now that was an idea.

for Victor E. Navarro
1947 – 2014

Our Hero

WHEN CAPTAIN MAPS CAME OUT OF NOWHERE to save that runaway bus full of blind nuns from careening into the river in the middle of town, we at the *Daily Reporter* had to admit: we were pretty relieved. With the advent of the 24-hour news cycle, the blogosphere, the decline of subscriptions, and creeping corporate cutbacks, we had taken to pumping up even the smallest story. We had just finished apologizing for the O'Dougherty kidnapping (LOCAL GIRL MISSING, PROBABLY MURDERED) after it was discovered she'd been visiting her grandmother for the weekend. That, on the heels of the school shooting debacle (they'd used cap guns in the eighth grade musical) and the clergy sex scandal (Father Michael, helping a woman in the confessional booth, had—allegedly—grazed her breast). We were anxious for real news. For one headline story we didn't have to sensationalize. We needed a legitimate sensation.

Those of us who were there described, in those first articles and op-eds, the sound of the Captain's approach before anything else. Rick in Sports wrote that it cracked over the voice of the announcer at the girls' slow-pitch game "like God hitting a softball." In the caption under the local weather map, Alex typed that it had sounded like "the mother of all thunderclaps." But it was Hal in Lifestyles who, though we didn't understand it at the time, perhaps said it best when he wrote that it was "a sound like a rip in the pants of the Universe." We ribbed each other in the break room and near the fax machine over our descriptions, accused one another of being excessively literary or purple in our prose. Those of us who hadn't seen the Captain appear heard so many stories about that moment that we soon spoke as though we had. We knew all the details: the sound, the ripple in the sky, the flash of green and blue leotard, the man hanging in thin air with the now-iconic cape—a map of the world—billowing behind him. The divisions between there and not-there, while at first tense and somewhat bitter, began to dissolve. We were united in our mission to report the truth. We pulled together in solidarity to deliver the news.

The first headlines were perhaps overly flattering. CAPED HERO SAVES NUNS, WORLD. SUPER MAN RESCUES, LOVES TOWN. LEOTARDS: PINNACLE OF SPRING FASHION? Our editor-in-chief Roberta sent them to press with a flick of her manicured fingers. Roberta, whose face only cracked to sneer at a misplaced adjective or improperly cited source, now smiled when we brought her stories of the Captain. She stopped smelling of gin and limes after lunch hour. She even ventured to pinch the butt of Topher, the intern, and gave him what he later described as a "flirty wink."

Our workdays grew longer. Because he had only appeared once, and only for a moment, our stories took on more hypothetical angles. Despite restrictions on overtime, we huddled together in our cubicles and speculated on his origins, his alter-ego, his motivations. Topher, being from a farm outside Topeka and possessing—according to some sources—a well-muscled physique, was immediately fingered as a suspect until it was confirmed he'd been at his desk playing Minesweeper and writing terrible things about our newsroom on his blog. Someone suggested the Captain might be some kind of super-soldier from the Air Force base on the edge of town. Someone else said he could be a geography professor from the university whose experiment gave him superpowers. One of the obit writers wondered aloud if perhaps he'd been bitten by a radioactive map. Everyone was a suspect. We eyed strangers on the street and kept notes on suspicious persons in the grocery store or church. We rifled through our husbands' dresser drawers and inspected the spaces under our brothers' beds. We tapped the walls of boyfriends' closets and garages, hoping for some hidden panel with a blue leotard and cape inside.

The newsroom buzzed. We held our breath, waiting for the next appearance of the Captain. We loosened our ties in what we thought was a cavalier and attractive way. We wore shorter skirts and started leaving our cardigans on the backs of our chairs. Roberta, who never wore anything but gray pantsuits, came to the office in red slacks and heels. When she sent article corrections back, she no longer signed her notes "EIC," replacing it instead with a swirly cursive "Roberta" punctuated with a lipstick kiss.

Then Captain Maps saved city hall from that meteor. The air rippled; that same heavy thunder-snap "like God rolling a perfect strike," as Rick wrote, cracked through downtown, and the Captain was flying above our little skyline, upper-cutting the big flaming rock back into space from whence it came. The crowd that had gathered cried out in joy. Children wept. The mayor, interviewed by our Lifestyles section, reported an impressive bulge in the front of the Captain's green briefs.

This was the news we needed. Our stories were picked up by the AP and Reuters, translated into a dozen languages. Photos from our very own photographer, Rashid, ran on the front pages of the *Times* and the *Post*. Our bylines were everywhere. We were booked on Fox, CNN, MSNBC,

ESPN-3, The Weather Channel. On national TV, with our makeup professionally done and our designer suits bought on credit, we gave our expert eye-witness accounts of Captain Maps. We were the media's front lines. The boots on the ground re: the world's first living superhero. On those news sets, or in our own conference room chatting via satellite uplink, we conducted ourselves like professionals. We imagined ourselves the Edward Murrows and Connie Chungs of a dawning era. The Captain was the biggest news of our lifetimes, and we were the commentators, the shapers, the voice.

Subscriptions soared. Our website crashed from so many hits. We wrote about Captain Maps from every angle, interviewed every witness, editorialized and hypothesized. When we ran out of things to write, we dug deeper. CAPED CRUSADER – HERO? we taunted. We needed to know. We needed to be the ones to break the story. It wasn't enough for the Captain to put our town—and our newspaper—on the map. Captain Maps was ours, right down to the name, which either Hal or Jeanine, our Business editor, had coined the day of his first appearance, depending on who you asked. Roberta had sent in the copyright on behalf of the paper. We were talking to toy companies about licensing. Some of us had started working on screenplays. On the walls of the newsroom, we hung posters of that first front page to remind us of our greatness, our bylines next to an artist rendering of the Captain in all his cape-waving comic book glory. When we dressed for work, we wore subtle combinations of green and blue, his unofficial fan club.

Weeks passed. Even if it hadn't been an election year, there were always wars and famines and water shortages and terrorist attacks. There was always news, but by then we weren't interested in the misery of the world. Without any new appearances from the Captain, newsworthy heroics, we were fading from the national eye. We'd ridden the Captain's cape into the limelight, and now he was shaking us off, back to our small-town beat. Jeanine, who'd written about the town's much-needed tourism surge, reported a drop in the local economy. Captain kitsch—balloons, T-shirts, cheap plastic dolls—washed from the gutters into the river, unbought and forgotten. Alex, in a last-ditch effort, rigged a spotlight on the roof, painted over with a blobby North and South America, shining it into the night sky for days until Roberta told him to stop wasting electricity.

Soon there were reports of the Captain saving people in India, Morocco, Papua New Guinea. We felt betrayed. More than one of us burst into tears near the photocopier. He had abandoned us. Captain Maps had been our exclusive, our hometown hero. Now he was saving the world while we were drowning. Some of us started taking dark alleys on our walks home. We kept to the worst parts of town, our phones ready to record our salvation. Hal was mugged and lost his phone and thirty dollars, but still the Captain never came.

It's hard to remember who had the idea first. Probably someone in obits. It was Hal, however, with a designer ski mask over his beautiful face, who stole the purse from that old lady. For days after, our front page read, CRIME SURGES – HERO DOES NOTHING. CITY UNDER SIEGE, CAPTAIN SHRUGS. SUPER DO-GOODER DISAPPOINTS. By that time, the world had forgotten our little city. The Captain was on the front pages of the *Times* and the *Post* and the *Tribune* and a dozen small-town papers from Caracas to Constantinople, but he wasn't on ours. Even in an era when news had become entertainment and truth in journalism was a quaint anachronism, our papers didn't sell. Letters to the editor filled our inbox, calling us exploiters, charlatans, villains. We weren't villains. We were only trying to sell print news in an era when everything had not only gone digital, everything was editorial—iNews, consumed to reinforce a worldview the reader already had. News didn't sell newspapers. Not anymore.

After that, we lost heart. Even the most interesting news story was couched in the blandest terms. We were the opposite of what we had been. After the Captain, nothing was sensational. Even the explosion at the chemical factory, a legitimate disaster, elicited the tame headline POOF AT CHEM PLANT, buried on page A3.

We were back in the red. Subscriptions flatlined, advertisers bottomed out. Roberta, in the grayest suit she owned, sucked on a cigarette in the middle of the newsroom and announced, bleary-eyed, that there would be cutbacks. Ed the Night Editor was forced to retire—we couldn't afford to keep the lights on after 5 P.M. Topher, though he wasn't paid, drank too much water from the cooler and had to pack up all his action figures he kept in his cubicle. On his blog, he called us all "fagsicles" and claimed he'd been "shit-canned." He posted a picture of himself peeing in the photocopier. Roberta, bottle of gin half empty on her desk, said we didn't have the money to sue. Or to fix the machine.

There were those of us, however, who were not deterred. Those of us who were reporters in our bones. We knew Captain Maps was our salvation. He was the only news that mattered. We stayed late, long after the lights had been shut off, our faces lit by the glow of our laptops. Our wives and boyfriends called, phones buzzing as we let them go to voicemail. Days went by without us seeing our kids. Stains blossomed on our skirts and khakis. Our clothes stank of sweat and cigarettes, our hair frizzed or flattened with grease. Most of us forgot to eat, subsisting on stale coffee and saltines from the break room. Together, independently, we started digging into the dark web, the underbelly of the information superhighway. We traced the Captain's movements, his sudden appearances and disappearances, triangulating locations based on where headlines featuring the Captain appeared. We found composite images of his face and body type and paid hackers, from our own savings accounts, to run illegal facial recognition scans. Between writing puff pieces for our website, clickbait like 31 REASONS CAPTAIN MAPS SUCKS (YOU WON'T BELIEVE NUMBER 5!) to generate ad revenue, we began feeding anonymous threats into every corner of the Internet—bomb scares, terrorist plots—and waiting to see if the Captain would show. Nothing worked. The posters of that first front page were still on the walls, but the eyes of the Captain's likeness were all X'ed out. Darts and pencils protruded from the globe on his chest.

To hide the stains, we started wearing black, like it was our own funeral. Black jackets, black leggings, black boots. It was almost a uniform, with the odd purple pinstripe or lime green socks when someone felt especially daring. Roberta took to brooding in her office at night, long after most of us had fallen asleep beneath our desks. Her pantsuits darkened from gray to charcoal, until finally she settled on a black leather number with high, padded shoulders.

When she shaved her head, some of us found it sexy. But the monocle was a little much.

We stopped calling each other by name. Instead, we'd say Weather Man, Ms. Gossip, The Obituarist. We called Hal The Mask even after he asked us not to. None of us were who we used to be; or we were, in a baser form.

Juiced up on cheap coffee, we huddled together in the darkness of the office, plotting. We hadn't put a print edition on newsstands in weeks. We'd stopped bothering with local stories, with wars, with politics, with the weather. Captain Maps was the only news. And anyway, we didn't have the money to pay our printing costs. The rent was overdue on the offices. Our corporate parent company had cut all ties. Our online advertisers were abandoning ship. We'd be evicted by the end of the month.

We needed a real story. We needed an exclusive. Our eyes ringed purple with exhaustion and eyeliner, we edged closer, pens at the ready, toward our final story: the unmasking of Captain Maps.

It didn't have to come to this. If the Captain had remembered us, if he had brought us with him in his journey to fame, if he had said thank you, he might have stopped us before we ever started. We had loved him, and he left us in the dust, small people in a small, flyover town.

Reports had been coming in for a while about strange

occurrences near the site of the chemical plant disaster. Frogs bursting into flame, birds disappearing in clouds of smoke. It was Roberta's idea to go. Our fearless editor-in-chief led us single-file to a delivery truck in the basement garage, monocle gleaming, leather pantsuit squeaking as she marched. We packed in, elbow to elbow, a mass of black fabric and body stink. For most of us, it was our first time out of the newsroom in weeks.

Whatever we were expecting at the chemical plant, no one predicted that the ooze would just be there, waiting. Getting through the chain-link fence had been easy enough, with Roberta's bolt cutters. The building itself was half demolished. Charred bricks littered the grounds. We crawled through a hole pasted over with yellow police tape and made our way inside.

Roberta tried it first. The ooze glowed, as one of us would note, "like the pink heart of God" in the darkness of the factory. Our editor-in-chief, muttering something about the Captain and the bitter taste of revenge, plucked the vial from the flame-scorched cabinet, and downed it like a shot of top-shelf gin. Our fists squeaked in their leather gloves as we tensed and held our breaths. We almost didn't notice when the alarm began to blare. Roberta shook violently, red warning lights reflecting on her shaved scalp. Her monocle clattered to the floor. Then she stopped and opened her eyes, the whites of them humming bright red.

She winked and a nearby chair burst into flames, and The Mask said maybe we had another breaking news headline after all. Roberta passed more vials around, and we all took a guzzle. What did we have to lose?

A kind of purple fog swirled around Hal, and Rick from Sports swelled up with muscle like a tumor with fists. Blue lightning crackled around Jeanine's fingertips. The rest of us, too, changed—black wings sprouted, skin turned green, ice swirled from fists frosted over. It hurt like hell, and some of us no longer looked human. It didn't matter. We hadn't felt human for a long time.

Every superhero has a weakness, but we weren't looking for Captain Maps' kryptonite. We only wanted his attention, to get the exclusive we were owed. Without knowing what else to do, we went back to the source. The first thing the Captain had deemed worthy of his attention in this world. The first time our hero unzipped space-time and swooped in to save the day.

By the time the SWAT team surrounded the office building that housed our dark and cluttered newsroom, the cops staying at least fifty yards away per Roberta's orders, the plan was in full swing. We would bring the Captain back. We would get our story. Helicopters buzzed over the roof. Spotlights splashed across the windows. The newsroom had been emptied of cubicles, and Roberta paced, shining in her leather pantsuit. The rest of us stood at the edges of the room, away from the windows, our gloved hands ready with pens, pads, and tape recorders. Hal wore his signature ski mask. The rest of us left our faces uncovered. We were unrecognizable, even to ourselves. The hostages were in the center of the room, weeping. They wore black too, for different reasons. If we wanted the Captain's attention, we needed something we knew he cared about. Even with Rashid's X-ray vision, it wasn't easy to kidnap a whole busload of blind nuns. But Roberta had a plan, and in the end, we found them all, even the one hiding in the confessional booth.

Now we had a headline: *Daily Reporter* Issues Challenge to Superhero – Blind Nuns Held Hostage. There was no story yet. We were writing it as we went. So all we printed was the headline, on the last of the pulp, and delivered it in the dead of night to the town's newsstands. It didn't take long for someone to realize it wasn't fake news this time. The nuns were gone. When the police chief finally called, Roberta clenched the phone in a leather-clad fist and told him we only had one demand. We wanted Captain Maps.

As the nuns wept, we rocked nervously under the X'ed-out eyes of our posters of the Captain. We fidgeted with our new powers. Puffs of smoke and flame bloomed and disappeared like defective fireworks. Ice shards fell and melted into puddles. Some of us phased in and out of this plane of reality. Trying to lock down his own exclusive and betraying all of us writers and editors, Rashid set up a hidden webcam and soon we were streaming live, waiting for Captain Maps to show. Within minutes, the video went viral. Later it would be used in trials and Senate hearings, but just then it was our deliverance: the pants of the Universe ripped, the spotlight-swept windows of the newsroom shattered in wild sprays of glass, and there among us, thick hands knotted into fists, brows furrowed beneath a simple blue mask, was our hero.

Even with superpowers, most of us were not brave. We didn't get into the news business to be heroes. We were writers, people who tapped keyboards and hid behind our words. Better journalists than us may brave battlegrounds and natural disasters, but we were a small-town news team, more comfortable writing about spelling bees than speeding bullets. There, face to face with the square chin and comic-book muscles of Captain Maps, we were thankful that our skirts and pants were black so no one could see the stains. But we smelled it. It smelled just like the Xerox machine.

In a blue-green flash that rustled loose paper and tousled our hair, Captain Maps was in front of Roberta,

globe-adorned chest puffed out and both fists triumphant-
ly on his well-shaped hips.

"Breaking news, ma'am," the Captain declared. "Your
reign of terror is about to be out of print."

On Rashid's secret webcam, all of this streaming
around the world. We didn't know it, but we were famous
again. For that moment, we were news.

Ms. Gossip fired the first question. The Mask began
shouting another even before she finished, the Obituarist
barking something over that. Soon it was a barrage, a hail of
inquisition. We had to know. This was our exclusive, finally
our one-on-one. We circled like jackals, forgetting about
the nuns and the police and how the Captain, powerful
beyond our comprehension, had once punched a meteor
back into outer space. Our gloves clenched around pens
and tape recorders, we asked everything we could think of,
hoping for some answer, some kernel of truth. Question
after question until we got to the important ones: What
did we do? Why have you forsaken us? Why are we not
worthy of being saved?

Maybe it was the heightened moment, or the frustration we felt as Captain Maps, stepping back as if struck
by boulders, failed to answer a single question. Around the
room, eyes and hands began to glow and smoke and catch
flame. Rashid snapped photos with bright flash, and the

spotlights kept up their rhythmic sweep, a frenetic strobe effect illuminating the darkened newsroom, the Captain's eyes white and dumbstruck behind his mask.

Later, as we attempted to write our articles and memoirs from our specially constructed underground cells, we would argue over who landed the first blow. Some of us agreed with Rick, The Muscle, that it was his giant fist delivering a left hook to the Captain's perfect jawline that started the melee. Others remembered Jeanine, a.k.a. Newsflash, blasting blue lightning through the newsroom like a bolt from the gods. But the most loyal of us knew the truth: It had been Roberta who started the fight, her eyes glowing hellish red and her whole shaved head catching flame. After his cape and briefs caught fire, it was over for the Captain. Sure, Rick's punch made him dizzy, Jeanine's lightning made his hair stand on end, and Hal's swirls of smog blinded him to the rest of our attacks. The rest of us, too, all contributed in our own way: sonic screams, ghostly teleport kicks, trembling daggers of ice and iron and bone. But it was our editor-in-chief who knew what kind of story the reading public would clamor for. What headline would sell a newspaper. Strutting forward in her bright red leather pantsuit, blowing her deadly kiss as the rest of us shouted queries like cub reporters, Roberta started the fire that would consume the world.

In the end, of course, the *Daily Reporter* didn't run the story. DEATH OF CAPTAIN MAPS ran on every front page across the globe, but not ours. By then, there was no *Daily Reporter*. Only us, in our cells, scratching our stories into the walls. In the articles that appeared the following day, written by reporters who were better than we ever were, or at least less prone to hyperbole, less loose with the facts, the blind nuns—who'd all escaped unharmed—offered their eyewitness accounts. The smell of smoke and sulfur. The shriek of our voices. The final boom like "the seven trumpets of Revelations," according to the Mother Superior.

When the police finally stormed the building, after the nuns had shuffled down the fire exit and Roberta had launched her kiss of death, the beginning of the end, they found us hunched over laptops, scribbling in our notepads, rewinding our tape recorders. At the center of the room, visible in the blue glow of our screens: a spattered mask, and a cape with a sigil of a map of the world, ragged and black with flame. By then, Captain Maps was only an obituary. We finally had our scoop. We had copy to deliver, news to report. As we tapped furiously at our keyboards, Roberta stood over us, snapping her fingers, small fires on her fingertips igniting and snuffing out.

The Collector

THE OLD MAN COULDN'T REMEMBER when the severed hands had first appeared. For years, they had arrived unbidden, usually in the morning, their wrists showing all manner of cleavage: the neat slice of a well-sharpened knife, rough-toothed edges left by dull saws, ragged remains chewed by the jaws of exotic predators. Each morning, neatly splayed on the welcome mat next to his morning paper, the old man would find them: severed hands, as regular as the sunrise.

At first, he'd thrown them out with the rubbish. They were severed hands, after all, of no use to anyone anymore, except perhaps students of medicine or the dark arts. He would put them straight into the outside can, in opaque plastic bags, so that his cat, Jeff, would not climb the bin in the kitchen and pick at the discarded flesh.

Over time, though, the hands had begun to interest him. Their manifold sizes and shapes, their uniquely ravaged wrists. Some wore thin gold bands or ornate jewelry inlaid with stones. Some were tattooed, others virginal and small, the hands of infants and children, now faded to a purple-brown or white-blue. He began to store them, a kind of grim collection, in glass jars labeled with the date of arrival in his precise print. The first jars lined the upper shelves of the broom closet, but over the years had spread into the rest of the house, often stacked three or four deep in the corners of unused rooms. There were men's hands and women's, the hands of old priests and stillborn babies, hands with extra fingers and hands with the fingers all cut down to nubs. There were hands with purple polish still on the fingernails, hands swelling around diamond engagement rings.

After a year or two of careful storage, with so many mysteries surrounding each jarred hand, the old man began his research. He scoured obituaries, subscribing to multiple newspapers, looking for any links to the newest arrival, drinking his morning coffee with a long pour of heavy cream. He never once caught the secret couriers of hands in the act, never glimpsed the shapes of their backs as they stole away to unknown quarters. Whenever he stayed awake, watching, no hands were delivered. His notes were always left untouched, no answers given to his many questions. The collection became not so much an obsession as a routine. It was like brushing his teeth or paying the power bill; just something to be done.

Jeff, his cat, was gray with one white paw in the back. It was the sixteenth cat named Jeff. Before that, they had all been Archibald or Sven.

The morning the strangest hand appeared, the old man had not yet brewed his coffee. Without the invigorating smell of dark-roast Sumatra—which he had specially shipped in bulk from the city market—the house stunk of formaldehyde and kitty litter and the old, dusty spice of a grandmother's floral-print couch. The old man opened his front door, bent to gather his papers, and sneezed. His sneeze spattered the strangest hand he'd ever seen on his stoop. It was small and grubby, smeared haphazardly with green paint. At its wrist, where it should've ended in some severance of flesh, it instead was attached to an arm, running into a black sleeve that was, itself, part of a black dress worn by a small girl dressed as a witch. A green plastic witch nose curled over her mouth, stuck to her face with elastic string, and a black mole had been drawn on her little chin. Somewhere, in the earliest jars, the old man thought he had the hand of a real witch, blackened by fire. It was one of his favorites, the fingers so long they reminded him of his mother.

"Trick 'r treat," the girl said. In her other hand—that was a revelation, two hands at once!—she held a burlap coffee sack, bulging at the bottom with mysterious bounty. She thrust her free hand forward. "Trick 'r treat."

"I'm sorry," said the old man. "What is it that you want? Chocolate pieces?"

Jeff wound himself through the saggy legs of the old man's trousers, purring against his ankles. The cat eyed the girl suspiciously, back arched, before scurrying back inside. "You're supposed to have treats," said the girl. "Those are the rules."

The old man stroked his mustache nervously. "But it's morning. Aren't these rituals typically a nocturnal affair?"

"A knocked kernel what?" The girl scratched her black hair where it met the rim of her pointed hat. "You have to give me a treat. Otherwise, it's tricks. And you wouldn't like the tricks. You'd be real sorry if I had to trick you."

There was no one with the girl, as far as the old man could see. No grinning adult waiting just off the porch, no rumbling vehicle at the end of his long, twisting walkway. "Where's your mom or dad?"

"I'm not telling a stranger."

"I don't have any treats." The old man looked back into the house cluttered with jars. The only things he had were the hands, which he could not give to the tiny witch. You couldn't distribute severed hands to children.

"I'll take one," she said.

"You will take one what?"

"I'll take one of those hands you got."

"They're not for treating," he told her. "They're something else."

The witch frowned, a dark curve of lip under her plastic nose. "You're asking for a trick. A real mean one."

The old man fumbled with his newspapers. "I'm sorry, small witch," he said, ducking into his foyer. "Good luck with your quest for treats."

As he slurped his coffee, he tried to read the obituaries, but he could not get his mind off the small girl in the witch costume. He tried to think of the last time he'd seen someone, anyone, even the newsboys who delivered his daily papers. It had to have been before the appearance of the first hand, which itself was a distant memory. Jeff mewled and scratched at the floral-print cushions, and the old man was too preoccupied to throw a shoe at him to make him stop.

What was she doing there, a little girl at his front door? Why him, after so long? He looked for the date in the upper corner of the front page. It wasn't even October. The equinox had only just passed, and the leaves on the trees outside were still dark, bitter hues of green. As he sat in the funereal silence of his parlor, something thumped against the front door, startling him so greatly that he dropped his coffee, the mug shattering in a mess of ceramic in the puddle of dark roast. The old man rushed to the door, grabbing the baseball bat he kept by the coat tree. Its aluminum was dented and dusty, but the old man still had a hell of a swing.

On the porch, exploded from impact, were the bright orange entrails of a pumpkin. A wet spatter of stringy pumpkin gut marked its point of collision on the door, and in the yard, black hat pointing straight up, was the little witch.

The old man lowered the bat, his hollow cheeks flushed. He felt at once both livid and foolish. He wasn't usually the sort to go around swinging a bat at children.

"Trick 'r treat," the witch called from the yard. She wasn't even hiding.

"Go away," said the old man. "Go home. Go find your mother."

"I tricked. Now you treat."

"I have no treats, small sorcerer."

"The next trick will be worse. It'll be a real bad one."

The witch raised her broomstick and threw it as far as she could, which wasn't far at all. But the old man understood the girl's frustration.

"I will find you a treat, Miss Witch," he said. He turned back toward the front door, the baseball bat dragging thump-thump up the porch steps. Inside, he searched everywhere for a candy bar or chocolate chip, for some ancient, dusty butterscotch in faded foil. All his cupboards held were coffee tins and canned beans. He looked behind his rows and stacks and shelves of hands, but behind them he found only more hands, each with its careful label, its history. He had nothing. Nothing but hands.

"I'll take one," came the girl's voice.

The witch was standing in his foyer, two hands holding the sack open for her prize.

"You are trespassing, small witch. You are being a bad little person. I should call the authorities and have you locked in a cell forever till you are just bones."

"You don't scare me. You're just an old sad person with a bunch of hands. You won't miss one. Just one."

It seemed reasonable. Just one of the multitude, of the jars and jars that crowded his dark house. Just one, he wouldn't miss it, would he? And if anyone came by, an angry father or nosy policeman or torch-toting mob, asking questions about the hand, he had his story straight, he knew that he was innocent of any wrongdoing. He had only collected them, had made sure they would not be lost or forgotten.

But which hand? Which would be least valuable to his collection? Which was redundant? None, of course. Each was unique. They had been the hands of people, after all, and no two people had the same hand, the same death. He closed his eyes, breathed in through the shag of his mustache, and chose a jar at random. He did not even look to see which it was. He marched it over to the witch and said, "Your treat, little beast," dropping the jar into the dark opening of her sack. It landed with a crunch, as if on dry leaves or paper wrappers or dead skin. In some corner of the house, Jeff mewled like a haunting.

The little witch clutched her sack shut.

"Happy trick-r-treat, mister," she said.

"You too, tiny conjurer."

As she strode out the front door and down to the winding walk, the sack dragged thump-thump as it hit each stair.

The witch was there again with the morning papers. This time she was dressed in a black cape, plastic vampire fangs poking from her frown and a deep widow's peak drawn in black makeup on her forehead. The little vampire held the same burlap sack, still too dark to see inside.

"Trick 'r treat."

The old man had yet to discover which of his collection she had blackmailed from him the previous day. He had spent the rest of it in agitation, reading his obituaries and listening to a long symphony on his phonograph, then switching to classic rock 'n' roll because the symphony was too morbid. Jeff had hidden himself away till evening, eating his Meow Mix furtively as the old man spooned beans from a can. The cat had disappeared again after dinner, and the old man sat alone, falling asleep in his chair with a Lifestyles page as an ersatz blanket.

The vampire repeated her request for treats, her extortion.

"You have taken the last of my treats, foul child," said the old man, and he slammed the door on the little girl without even grabbing his newspapers.

Knocking again, then unintelligible little girl shouts. Within moments, tiny hands were rubbing soap on his windows. When he stormed out the front door, bat in hand, he discovered toilet paper streamers draping every support and rafter of his porch. A dozen rolls had been unspooled, hung like parchment sausages in a paper slaughterhouse. The vampire girl stood just beyond the mischief with her cape up like bat wings.

"I am calling the authorities!" the old man spat. Saliva flew as he shouted. "You will be arrested and tried and sentenced!"

He hurled the baseball bat in anger, watching it bounce off the railing of the porch and clattering hollowly to rest beside the welcome mat. As he slammed the door again, the jars of hands rattled in their corners and he knew he would not call the authorities or anyone else. They would take his hands. He would be arrested and tried and sentenced. They would send Jeff to an animal shelter or let him fend for himself in the mean streets, half feral.

In desperation, he grabbed the nearest jar and tossed it onto the porch. He sat against the door, listening to the jar roll across the wood and down the stairs—thump-thump. A rustle of grass, or a vinyl cape.

"Happy trick-r-treat, mister!"

A long time later, in the dead silence of the afternoon, he retrieved his papers and brewed his coffee, reading the obits in the hazy light of the soaped windows.

The next day she was a mummy. Long strips of canvas dyed pale brown in boiled tea wrapped her spindly arms and legs, and crisscrossed her face, leaving her eyes and mouth free. She feigned a dead stare and stood with her arms out stiff, drawling "Trick 'r treat" in a zombie voice.

He dropped one of the jars in her sack without a word, picked up his papers, and went to pour his coffee. As he read, Jeff watched him from his perch on a stack of hand jars, the cat looking as disappointed as a cat can look.

"What was I supposed to do, Jeffrey?"

The cat moved its tail.

"I can't do that. The small beast would be missed. Surely some parent or guardian knows she is out playing this game. They would find the body."

Jeff licked his teeth.

"Jeffrey, that is hideous. Even for you. I will not feed a little girl to a cat."

Blink.

"Or put all of her parts in jars."

Blink.

"It is not the same, Jeffles. The hands arrived according to their own cosmic destiny. I didn't murder them and save their parts."

Tooth lick.

"I know they would. Anyone would. I got myself into this, keeping them. Any sane mob would say I killed them and boil me alive."

At night, before bed, he brushed his hand along the rows of severed hands, licking the corners of his mustache. He plucked a small jelly jar from the bunch, which had a pale infant's hand inside. For years it had been a part of his collection. A small new life, ended before the hand could touch anything useful or interesting, before it could write or punch or pluck a harp string. He looked at the rest of his jars, all the hands and lives. They felt less like a collection then. They felt more like shame.

The little girl kept coming. Each morning, instead of a new severed hand, was a monster or a pirate or a Martian, her sack dark and open and never seeming to fill. Each day the collection of jars got one jar smaller. The old man never looked to see which of the hands he gave her. He didn't want to know whose life he was giving away, which person was victim to the child's game. He fell into a new routine: brew coffee, give a hand, retrieve the papers, and read. Jeff grew more reclusive, keeping to the many shadows of the house. Years passed, and Jeff died underneath the bed. The old man buried him in the back garden. Soon after, in a nearby barn, he found a scrawny calico. He named her Jeff, too. He'd gotten used to the name. The girl trick-r-treated as the years fell away, never getting taller, never repeating the same costume, but all of them slapdash and homemade, with cardboard swords and red hoods made from table cloths. The old man stopped reading the obituaries. There was no reason; there were no more hands to research, no labels to affix. He listened to his records and played lonely games with Jeff, who was less talkative than her predecessor. This cat was just a cat, and when she died, he buried her beside the old Jeff, but he didn't blubber or fidget with his mustache, didn't shed any tears.

On the last morning, the old man went to the broom closet to fetch the girl's daily jar. He found only one jar on the shelf, the very first, the dustiest and oldest of all the jars he'd collected. It was an average hand, too aged and mummified to even tell the race or sex. It was simply a hand, very old, with a label whose ink had faded over the long decades of storage.

He found the girl on the porch as he had for years

now. She should have been in college, or a young mother, or a powerful woman asserting herself in a strange and hungry world, but she was still six or seven and in a skeleton costume, cutouts of bones from a white sheet sewn to a black ballet suit. The girl was even wearing ballet slippers, and she pirouetted and smiled, her face whited out and drawn into skull form with a black grease pencil.

"Trick 'r treat," she said. She pulled up her sack and held it out.

"It is the last treat," said the old man as he dropped the jar into the bag. "I have nothing but beans left. And if I give you those, I will starve and die."

The skeleton closed her sack and twirled. "I took dance lessons. Want to see?"

"No."

But the skeleton wasn't listening. She was dancing. On the tiptoes of her slippers, she moved across the creaking boards of the porch, a ballet of bones. She danced so gracefully, so fluidly, the old man felt a twitch at the corners of his mustache, the unfamiliar spasm of a smile. She danced and reached, and suddenly she was whirling the old baseball bat as she arabesqued and petite-cabrioled and fouettéd over the boards. The old man was smiling, somehow smiling, his house empty behind him and the small skeleton girl flitting beautifully with the rusted aluminum in both of her small bone hands. Pirouette, arabesque, plié, and the bat arced upward in one fluid motion he didn't even see. Bone and flesh crunched. Teeth rattled against the wooden porch like rolled dice. The old man's body fell backward into the foyer, dark blood pooling beneath his collar.

The little skeleton dropped the bat and shuffled en-pointe toward her sack. It was heavy with the decades of jars in there, and the hands and bodies of centuries past. She rooted around a while before she found the knife she kept for moments like this. Pirouette, fouetté. The old man was at her feet, his eyes still open but watching nothing. She crouched and began her work.

When she was finished, she dropped the stump of the old man's arm and tied the thin, soft hand carefully with a black ribbon, stuffing it into a special pocket of her old sack. She made a note to remind herself to label it when she got home, the sack dragging thump-thump as she made her way back to the forest.

The Number 9 Train

In the morning, he left before Yuki woke. She was still curled at edge of the bed, her thin back like a wall. At the cloudy, brass-framed mirror she'd bolted to her dresser, Ethan put on yesterday's clothes, Windsor-knotted the same blue tie. The room around him felt like a museum. Since her divorce, she'd been stocking it full of ancient furniture, each dilapidated piece bought for next to nothing at one of the bazaars in the worker districts. A phonograph, a plain birch bookshelf, a headboard made from an old door. Nothing with an advertising screen or built-in digitune stream. Not a microchip among them. And Yuki, breathing ribs barely moving: a wax statue to complete the anachronistic display. He did not leave a note or kiss her goodbye.

The city outside was utilitarian gray. Towers reached into the underbellies of clouds. It wasn't raining yet. Too early for breakfast, too late to go back to his apartment to change, he walked to the train station. The only Downtown route running then was the Number 9. Even before descending to the platform, he knew this. Since he'd met Yuki—five months, almost six—he had started taking the Commuter Express, but after two years of riding the 9, its schedule was intuitive.

Ethan bought his ticket, milled among strangers and floating holographic billboards—ads for bachelorette cruises and lust gurus—thinking of nothing except Yuki. He should have left a note. Or stayed, woken her, made love half-asleep in the shower and shared a bagel on the walk to the Number 7 Express, its bright plastic capsule too sterile for grudges or lingering arguments, and Yuki's head would rest on his shoulder as she talked about next weekend's bazaar, the stained-glass lamp she hoped to find.

Except she wouldn't have said a word. She would have shrugged him off in the shower, toasted her own bagel and thrown half away. She wouldn't forgive him yet, not that easily. At dinner, she had insisted on paying the bill again. He thanked her in a low, spiteful tone, left the restaurant without waiting for her. On the train ride back to her apartment, they'd fought. She said he always kept one eye on the door, and she'd seen him flirting with the waitress again, did he think she wouldn't notice? He kept a part of him secret, walled off from her, why wouldn't he let her in? She made him feel useless. She seemed so complete, happy, unbroken. Back at her place, it wasn't make-up sex. Just a tactile extension of the argument. When she fell asleep, too angry to even roll toward him in the uncertain consciousness of her dreams, he looked around at the dark shapes of strange furniture and wondered why he stayed.

Ethan looked around the station. Beside a holographic bottle of zero-calorie beer, two women stood with jackets folded over their arms, talking politely, their heavily shadowed eyes scanning the crowd of men near the ticket kiosk. One was brunette and mousy, close to his age, he guessed—late twenties. The other, platinum blonde and older, breasts straining against her blouse like warheads. Train regulars probably, spotting potential Meeting Room partners. Ethan flicked the ticket against his palm absently, checked his wrist for the time, finding only his bare forearm. He'd been in such a hurry to leave, he forgot his watch again on Yuki's dresser; he'd even banged his knee against an open drawer in the half-light. Yuki liked to brag that the dresser was real wood, and the peeling mint-green paint showed grain as if to prove it. A four-sided digital clock hung from the station's domed concrete ceiling: the train was two minutes late. The blonde was staring at him now, one eyebrow arched like a question mark. Yuki was asleep, or not, realizing he was gone, moving alone through her morning routine. Ethan blushed a little, didn't smile back.

The train arrived with a hydraulic whisper. Women shuffled first into its wide airlock doorway, several men behind them, Ethan last. As the airlock hissed shut, he turned and touched the cold chrome door as if looking for a doorknob, an exit button. Through its round porthole, the brightness of the station blurred and disappeared, giving way to the black of the tunnel, then to the gray ellipse of morning.

He stuffed his jacket into a locker in the first car, took the numbered key from its lock. He could still smell Yuki in his shirt collar, sweet sweat and jasmine oil. The women had already moved into the dining car. Two men in suits, locking their briefcases in nearby lockers, compared the women's breast sizes, determined the blonde more fuckable. They could have been Ethan and Pradeep two years ago, fresh out of design school, before Ethan started at the firm, before Pradeep's marriage. When they began riding, they had made a pact—only six months, a few lays on the way to internships at mid-range urban-design centers, what could it hurt? Six months, then it would be time for real women, real jobs, real lives. Now in infrequent e-mails, Pradeep bragged about his family, sent artsy black-and-white photos of his two baby daughters. He ribbed Ethan about the train. He said no one ever found true love on their morning commute. When Pradeep met his wife and moved to one of the outer districts, Ethan continued to ride the train out of habit, most days only collecting business cards with cell-phone numbers scribbled on the backs—hearts in place of zeroes—promises of maybe-next-time. Sometimes, if he called, they'd meet in an off-train bar, go to her apartment and open another bottle, walk separately to the station the next morning, pretend not to recognize each other after that.

In the dining car, plush, high-backed booths lined each side of the walkway, creating private nooks for couples, for the odd troll here and there drinking alone. The red tint in the car's recessed lighting made Ethan think of a speakeasy, what he imagined the basement bars of Downtown must be like. Maybe that weekend, their argument far behind them, he would take Yuki to one, whisper passwords to gold-toothed bouncers through unmarked steel doors. Dress up like an ancient mobster and his moll: rented zoot suit and flapper dress. They could call each other by old-fashioned names. Edward and Margaret. Albert and Francesca.

Six months. How had it been that long? He wanted to blame Yuki, but she was the one who wanted to take it slow from the beginning. Her first marriage had been rushed, just out of college, a four-year spat of violent fights and infidelity. She didn't want to make another mistake. Her left ring finger still showed a thin, pale ring of skin. He'd noticed it the first time they'd had sex—in her bed, a month into the relationship, surrounded by the ghosts of old furniture. Each caress had been deliberate and measured, as if the universe had slowed itself in order not to rush that moment. Nothing like the frenetic desperation of the train. The skin on her finger reminded Ethan that she would never be only his, and in the weeks after, he had felt a desperate need for her, to enter her and own her. They fell into routines. He promised ridiculous things, a future together that made her embarrassed and silent. One week turned into two turned into twenty. The movement was so seamless, he didn't notice. Now he slept at her place most of the week, kept a coffee pot on her counter, next to her basket of green tea. When she asked why they didn't spend more time at his apartment, he kissed her, said her bed was more comfortable.

The train stopped and idled. Ethan watched commuters pass the windows as he waited for the train to resume its spiraling loop through the city and its endless districts. Yuki would be awake by now, his side of the bed cold. Only his watch on the dresser would prove he had been there. He checked his pockets for his phone, remembered it was in his jacket, in the locker. If she called, he couldn't answer. He couldn't call to apologize. Did he even want to? He stumbled past the booths, toward the back of the car. Men and women sat behind uneaten bagels and full mugs of coffee, gulping mimosas and Bloody Marys with too much pickle juice. They praised the virtue of private enterprise, the corporate efficiency of the transit system. One remarked on the economic viability of the civil union ban, another promoted commercial sponsorship of sexual communes. All of it, noise.

"Getting back your train legs?" said the man in the booth. He sat alone in the red shadow of the speakeasy lights. He was balding, more gray than black in his beard, and the bulk beneath his suit suggested a once-muscular form. Ethan pegged him for a troll, one of the lonely middle-aged men who'd wasted too many years on quick train fucks, counting the seconds with some too-young secretary in a Meeting Room. Always holding out for *better* until they're too old to get *good enough*. Pradeep had coined the term. Trolls smelled desperate, like too much knockoff bazaar cologne. Something about him was familiar—Ethan had probably seen him on the train before. Most riders were regulars.

"Just riding," Ethan said. "Nostalgia's sake."

"Escape's sake is more like it," the man said. "I've been there. Sleeping in, eating a balanced breakfast, taking the Express. What's her name?"

"She takes the 7," Ethan said.

The man smiled, and his grip tensed on a sweating tumbler of dark alcohol. The glass was heaped with ice—one of the bartenders' tricks.

"And how is your little geisha doll?" the man said. "Enjoying her new office?"

"Excuse me?" Ethan said.

"Don't remember me, do you?" the man said. "I guess you wouldn't. We barely met, at some function your geisha no doubt dragged you to."

Now Ethan recognized him. Part of the firm's upper-management. A name with a Viking sound. Eriksen. Svensen. Larsen. That was it: Larsen the Letch. He'd given the keynote at the firm's fourth-quarter gala. Yuki had left the room. When Ethan found her outside, she told him Larsen had offered her a promotion in exchange for a week at a mistress resort in Barcelona. She confessed that she'd considered it. Instead, she was promoted to a different department, on merit, but according to office gossip, photos of Larsen and some other upwardly mobile executive at the resort's spa had made it to his wife, along with pictures of him on the train. Apparently he had kept them away from the transit corporation. There were rules against affairs, fines and blacklisting for transgressors. Corporate law was clear: Singles Only. Affairs, swingers, marriage-seekers, please see the train in your category.

"She knows I'm here," Ethan said. He wondered if she had eaten breakfast yet, whether her tea was heating as she showered off his sweat.

"Sure she does," Larsen laughed, exposing a row of

perfectly capped teeth. "Like I give a fuck." He took another gulp from his glass. "You should keep moving on a train like this. One car to the next, till you're in back, in a room. Eyes on the prize." Larsen glanced at the couples in the other booths, lowered his voice. "I have my eye on this redhead from the Uptown stop. Had her screaming gibberish in a room last week. Hoping for a reprise. Skinny chick, tits like God's angels. Not the prettiest, a little knobby, but the beautiful ones are always dead fish. If the face isn't great, she feels like she needs to work for it."

None of the women near them seemed to hear. Ethan mumbled a good luck, positioning himself near the door.

"The fucking absentee is incredulous," Larsen said to no one in particular. "Doesn't think I can bed the redhead. Off the train for a few months, he thinks he still knows how things work. What do you bet, a day's wages? You can afford it, what with the geisha doll's VP salary." Larsen leaned back into the shadow. His glass was empty except for its collapsing structure of ice. He saluted with it anyway. "Hope you get the room next to us so you can hear her. Sounds like she's speaking in tongues." He thumped the glass on the table and called into the booth's intercom for another scotch. Ethan took his cue to leave. With a half-smile and another good luck, Ethan pushed into the bar car.

The crowd was bad: shoulder-to-shoulder singles

sweating through the sleeves of their work shirts. The air vibrated with conversation and air conditioning and digitized piano jazz. Ethan wedged into an open corner at the bar. The bartender snapped her fingers.

"Irish coffee," Ethan said. "Extra Irish."

"We don't do that anymore," she said. "Corporate restrictions."

"Then whatever isn't restricted. Please."

She set a mug in front of him a moment later. He blew the steam, then sipped, mouth numbed by the initial burn. He tasted only French roast, but he hoped the coffee would calm his nerves anyway. Even if Larsen kept his mouth shut, one of Yuki's friends or interns could be in the crowd. He imagined charming them into a Meeting Room, making them complicit. Trusting them to feel the right amount of guilt to keep quiet. Except that was ridiculous. He didn't want them or a room. He wanted—he didn't know what he wanted. To punish Yuki? To prove something? Maybe only to feel a familiar motion. Things moved—trains, elevators, clock hands. He knew they moved, but they moved imperceptibly, as if teleporting from one point to the next.

Digital numbers ticked down time on the mirror behind the bar. Still half an hour to Downtown Station. The gradient of gray-black-white beyond the window signaled another stop. Ethan braced himself against the handrail, anticipating the brakes. He surveyed the crowd for the women he'd seen in the station. The mousy brunette twitched her face at a short man with a fire-red beard. The blonde wasn't there. He looked for Larsen's redhead, examined bodies for model proportions. The opposite of small, soft Yuki. An old feeling lurched inside his chest. One that told him these women, pretending to be drunk on cocktails that were nine-tenths orange juice and wearing too much makeup for a day at the office, were second-rate. Temporary. Not real. The day he met Yuki, he had bored himself all morning with an online-librarian, didn't even bother to go to a Meeting Room when she offered. They traded cards, but he de-boarded Downtown feeling defeated. As he pushed the button for floor 20 in the firm's lobby elevator, Yuki hobbled toward him dragging a canvas bag of blueprints, a broken sandal hanging from her teeth by its strap. Ethan held the door. She talked for twenty floors about nothing he could remember as she unsuccessfully tried to rethread the sandal. He watched the floor numbers light in sequence, absently cataloguing her faults—her chatter, her expensive broken heel (clumsy *and* bourgeois), her chic wire-rim glasses, the slight space behind her left canine tooth, thin lips, obvious eyebrows, small breasts. She was still beautiful despite all of this. For the rest of the morning, he ignored blueprint deadlines and conference calls. The next day, the train felt like a set piece in a black-and-white movie, the city a projection on a screen outside its windows. He sat alone at one of the booths, waving off women's drink offers. At the firm, he loitered in the lobby until he saw her approach the elevator, waiting all twenty floors before he asked her to dinner.

He leaned against the bar and drank the coffee down to the dregs. If he had any buzz, it was only caffeine. The whiskey's proof was too low to matter. He looked for the redhead again, spotting a possible candidate at the other end of the bar. Her unnatural fire-red waves were held in a tight bun with a pair of chopsticks. If she was Larsen's gibberish girl, he had her wrong. Skinny suggested triangles—a body of jutting bones and apexes, like all architects' wives. This redhead was tall and slender, sinewy, probably a runner, her hipbones barely straining the fabric below the beltloops of her pencil skirt. Ethan began to wonder whether she really sounded like a rapturous born-again or whether the gibberish were a language Larsen was just too ignorant to recognize.

The red numbers on the mirror counted down. Conversations adopted subtle urgency. The rhythm of the crowd pulsed. Even the jazz sped up. Men and women huddled together, smiling too hard, milking the last of their two-drink limit. Ethan edged through them until he was arm-to-arm with the redhead.

"Buy you a drink?"

Her glass was half empty.

"At my limit," she said. She was pretty enough. Her teeth gapped in the front, conspicuously if not unattractively. He searched her voice for any trace of accent. He wanted to guess she was Norwegian, but he knew he was inventing that. Still, he could hear her gasping prayers to Thor as they hammered pelvises on the train's stain-resistant sheets. His stomach somersaulted. He had left Yuki's without showering, still had her on him from the night before. He was worse than Larsen. Larsen, at least, had nothing but the train and a broken marriage and fleeting tongue-speaking redheads.

"Tahitian martini," said the redhead. She turned, as if talking to someone else, and her breast brushed his arm. The gesture could have seemed accidental in a different context. She added, with another smile, "If you can get one."

At that, he fell into the familiar script. He raised his hand for the bartender and ordered the drink. The redhead held out a long-fingered hand. "I'm Alyssa."

He noticed the pale skin around her left ring finger.

"What do you do, Alyssa?"

"I don't do small talk," she said.

The bartender set the drink in front of him before sliding his cash from the bar top. He waited for her to leave before handing the highball to Alyssa. Raising an imaginary glass, he said, "Here's to no small talk."

She laughed and tapped his finger with the rim of the glass. A note in the pitch of her laugh was sad, or mocking, or both. He was suddenly aware of the dull pain in his knee where he'd hit Yuki's dresser and the naked space on his watchless wrist. He was aware of the sharp elbows of the crowd, the spiraling miles of city, the silent magnetic rails beneath their feet. Of Yuki walking to the station alone and Pradeep kissing his daughters good morning and Larsen waiting for a second scotch. Of the weight in his chest, his lungs shrinking and ballooning against his ribcage, more rapidly than towers whipped past the windows, everything and everyone moving all at once, not even buildings standing still.

"Are you okay?" she said. She sounded nothing like Yuki.

"Yeah," he said. He loosened his tie and shifted his shoulders for elbow room.

"You're spilling my drink."

He looked: a puddle of pink alcohol was dripping from her hand onto his shoes.

"Come on," she said.

When she took hold of his arm, he didn't pull away. She led him through the dwindling bar crowd, through the door at the back of the car, into two empty bar cars before the first Meeting Room section. They followed stumbling couples who twisted door handles until one opened. The redhead led him into a room and locked the door. Inside, she wrestled his tie over his head. She slid out of her skirt and folded it on the microfridge. He sat on the bed in his socks and boxers, watching her body perform mechanical motions. Unbuttoning. Unfastening. Unfamiliar. The room was windowless. Without the passing city, it felt disconnected, immovable.

"Relax, okay? We only have fifteen minutes."

She pushed him onto the bed and plucked the complimentary condom from beside the pillow mints. While she rolled it on, he stared at the digital countdown on the ceiling mirrors, numbers shaded with naked reflections of the redhead and himself. Shadows cut seams around his eyes and mouth. Maybe a trick of the lighting— it was hard to see. She ground herself on him, back and forth, never speaking anything but English. Short grunts of *Uh-huh* and *Ohyeah*. He didn't move. The numbers sped them closer to Downtown, to offices and deadlines and the rest of their lives. He closed his eyes and remembered the afternoon Yuki bought the dresser. Its bulk between them, they stumbled away from the bazaar through one of the project districts, passing the cracked mirror windows of an Uptown apartment tower. Yuki watched their broken reflections for the entire block and, without irony, said she wouldn't mind living there. They carried the dresser another seventeen blocks, breaking halfway for beer at a sidewalk café. As her bottle sweat a ring onto its surface, Yuki ran her fingertip along the contours of the drawers. She wiggled her fingernail in the splintered holes where handles were missing. They had only been dating a month. "I wish I had a house full of old junk like this," she said. "Any time you come into a room, it's like traveling back in time." That night, after they made love for the first time, he imagined a house built of broken-down furniture, a lean-to of warped dressers and hope chests, the two of them together in Yuki's knobby post bed, under a canopy of rags.

"Did you come?"

The redhead was kneeling on the bed, off of him, examining the shrunken condom. The countdown beeped above them—five minutes to Downtown.

"Hey, did you come? Do you want me to finish you off?"

The top floor of that Uptown tower could be theirs. Each room furnished in a different era: ancient claw-footed chairs, orange shag loveseats, redundant sets of card-catalogue drawers. He could sign the lease today, surprise her, the act itself enough of an apology, he wouldn't have to say the words. Watch the orange sun sink behind the skyline every afternoon, raise two sons to Pradeep's two daughters, make love in the morning before their commute together. Wasn't that what love was? What else could it be? Yuki would be at the station now, alone on the platform with her bag of blueprints. The Express would arrive any minute, a perfect white bullet, and she would board separate from the crowd, sit in an empty section, without him, because she did not need him. She was too whole.

"You should get dressed," she said. "We're almost there." The redhead slipped back into her skirt, wedged her feet into matching red heels. "Thanks for that. It wasn't much, but thanks. Maybe some other morning."

The door locked automatically behind her, and Ethan snapped off the condom. He checked the microfridge for a bottle of anything, but looking at the rows of tiny, overpriced bottles, he took a cube from the ice tray instead. It tasted of latex and cold, the taste of nothing. As he lay back, he felt the brakes squeeze the train to a stop, and the time on the mirrors rushed toward zero.

Robot on a Park Bench

1

THE ROBOT'S KNEES HAD RUSTED in the autumn rains. He lifted each leg, exercising the oxidation out of the joints. According to his barometric sensors, there would be precipitation within the hour. More complications for his joints. A silicon frame, like the one the facility gave to newer models, might have been preferable: lightweight and unrustable. But everything has its flaws. In any case, he hadn't been given the choice.

As he walked through the park, his square, heavy feet sunk into the earth. Dirt clotted in their ridges of tread, which he would have to dig out later, before re-entering the facility.

A man was sleeping on one of the benches. The robot couldn't feel cold—a slowness in his metal body, maybe, but not the chill—though he knew the park was cold.

His temperature gauges read 0.6 centigrade. Factoring the man's approximate age, weight, the alcohol content level on his sleeping breath, and the relative thickness of his camouflage blanket, and assuming temperatures and all other variables remained constant (the man did not wake up, no one added a thicker blanket), the robot calculated that the man would be dead in five hours.

With his joints squeaking and grinding as they were, the robot was sure the man would wake, but he only stirred and shifted onto his side, giving himself another fifteen to seventeen minutes, approximately, to live.

By the time he reached the carousel, the robot was tired. He had been tired, in fact, for a very long time. Perhaps he had been programmed tired. There were no recorded dates in his memory banks that were not tinged with some degree of weariness, some exhaustion with the world and his role in it, though what that role was he still did not seem to know.

The carousel's lights and music were off, and a heavy green tarpaulin had been hung from hooks in its ornamented roof to shelter the wooden animals from winter. Beyond the carousel, the river trickled toward the Water Power dam, the falls, and, after [*Processing…Processing…*] 825.06 kilometers of lakes and reservoirs and dams, the ocean.

The robot stomped his treaded feet on the sidewalk

but the dirt stuck. His knees were stiff. The barometer was dropping. He settled onto a bench, up the bank from the river, where two small birds wrestled over a lollipop stick. The birds' movements were so quick, they seemed incomplete, unfluid, as if from a film that was missing essential frames. The birds hopped from moment to moment on their lithe, brittle legs, the stick like a thread between them.

2

When the first snowflake fell on the park, it settled on the robot's heavy, bolted jaw and froze in place. By then, the park seemed almost empty: the dying homeless man, an old woman dragging a little flat-faced dog, a jogger in gray sweats with white wires in her ears. Across the river, two park workers were raking leaves into big black bags. A young man with a beard walked his bearded dog past them and onto the footbridge. The bearded man and the bearded dog: somewhere in the banks of the robot's circuitry played an old television laughtrack. The two bearded animals turned toward the river, the smaller beast sniffing loose duck feathers on the concrete. They passed the robot without realizing he was there; he was part of the landscape.

"Please," the robot said. "Ask your dog not to urinate on my foot."

The man nearly jumped out of his skin [*Processing… "jumped out of his skin," an idiom appropriate for the sensa-*

tion of fright/surprise]. The robot had been integrating the idioms he overheard in the facility, and he prized his ability to use them in context.

"I have problems with rust," said the robot. "It is not pleasant."

"Sorry," the man said. He jerked the leash, and the dog, already finished, wiggled off toward a garbage can to sniff. "I'm sorry about that. I didn't see you."

The robot tilted its skinny bucket head and shook the pee off its leg. "It's all right," the robot said. Its voice played like a vinyl recording from a speaker in its mouth, and when it spoke, it opened its jaw wide to project the sound. "I have problems with rust. There are problems with my joints. The bolts, you see."

"Is this a joke?" the man said.

"Is what a joke?" the robot said.

"Am I on camera?"

"I'm sorry," the robot said. [*Processing…Processing…*] "That does not correspond with my definition of 'joke.'"

The man laughed. The robot's mouth opened again. This time, the laughtrack played through its speaker. The man stopped laughing. The robot continued for a moment too long, then its jaw slammed shut.

"My data suggests that it is appropriate to express amusement when another is expressing amusement."

The robot noticed a car pass the park without its

headlights on. It shrunk into the white horizon, its back lights flashing briefly red before it turned a corner, away from the river. Snow was settling on the robot's arms and legs. It fell in spirals over the river and the carousel and the other benches lining the sidewalks. It was collecting now, thin sheets and clumps of white over the whole park, the city.

"Your data is probably right," the man said. "This snow might be a problem too. For your joints. It's really coming down."

"I like the river," the robot said. He picked one snowflake out of the millions and followed its arc into the icy surface of the river. "Do you watch it much?"

"Do I what?"

"Is this grammar not correct? My data assures me this verb is correct."

"No, it's fine. I don't usually go around watching rivers. It's cold."

"Minus zero-point-seven centigrade."

"Right."

The robot gestured toward the water. The articulate fingers and wrist whirred with the working of gears. "Can you see that?"

"See what?"

"A bird is dying."

"I don't see anything."

3

The man with the dog asked him where he was from, and was he lost? The robot wasn't lost. He had a GPS uplink in his chest. The engineers and technicians, if they had use for him, would page his uplink and convey the exact coordinates of the next intelligence test or hardware upgrade or military demonstration. Increasingly, because of the newer models, the more human-looking prototypes with their moving latex faces and silicon frames, they did not have a use for him. For now, he was just taking a walk. He'd been taking walks for months, each one a little further from the facility. From the satellite maps, he had known a river ran nearby. A runoff from the mountains, with a big rocky falls at the heart of the city.

He was watching the river now. The river and the people and the snow: the world with all its moving parts.

"The snow is pleasant."

"I guess so."

In the storage room at the facility, two striped cats caught the mice that escaped from the laboratory cages, and when the mice were gone, it was the robot's job to feed them tuna from cans he held in his palm. The technicians had named them George and Gracie, though they were both females, the robot discovered, and he had secretly taken to calling the other Georgia. He liked that, having a secret. He liked learning that he could keep secrets.

He could feel the snow's weight now. The mean temperature of his body had lowered, though the networks of circuit boards throughout his head and abdomen were running at safe temperatures. He calculated that, if he did not move from the bench, and if all other variables remained constant, his functions would begin to slow in less than two hours. He didn't think he would mind. The river was still moving. The man and the dog were still there.

As long as he wasn't asked directly. That was it. The technicians and the engineers never asked by what name he called the smaller cat. He was not compelled to tell them. They did not ask where he went when he wasn't in the storage room or why he never associated with the new models. When they did ask about the rust, he said it had developed from the oxidation process that resulted from the chemical fusion of water and iron. Technically, that had been a factual response.

The robot calculated that, as long as he was never asked directly, he could keep a secret indefinitely.

"My girlfriend is going to wonder where I am," the young man said. "The dog is getting cold."

"Yes," the robot said. "The dog will die in three-point-two hours, if variables remain constant."

"Right. I don't want him to do that."

"That would be unpleasant."

The robot leaned forward to pet the bearded dog. The dog made a sound of fright and bit the robot's flat steel hand. This, it seemed, caused the dog more confusion than pain.

"He doesn't like strangers much. He's starting to go blind."

"If only he could be upgraded."

"Right," the man said. "Don't stay too long."

"How long is too long?" the robot said. It wasn't a question for the man.

"Long enough to freeze, I guess. To cause frostbite, or whatever. Frost-rust."

"Yes," the robot agreed. "That would be too long."

4

On the telephone poles outside the park, there were no Missing Robot fliers. Cars rolled through Downtown, churning dirt and gravel through the new snow. The man and the dog trudged through drifts of white toward home. Snowflakes continued their analog whirl, falling faintly and faintly falling upon all the living and the digital.

5

The robot's sensors noted the darkening of the sky over the park. They measured spectroscopics and lumenoscopics and the gradual shutdown of the robot's own secondary functions. Data relayed from chip to chip, in whatever network of copper and silica comprised the robot's consciousness. Now, under thick clumps of wet snow, he did not bother to move his limbs, and anyway, the joints had been frozen for an hour. He watched the river move until it was too dark to see, or until his optics ceased to operate, he did not know which. He listened to the water until his aural sensors froze over. The temperature kept dropping. He sat on the bench in the darkness of himself and waited for the last of his primary functions to cease, for the moment when he would no longer be aware of moments.

Who would feed Georgia and Gracie? The little cans of tuna on the floor of the store room: who would open them, if not him? That had been his job. A job is a kind of purpose, a reason to exist, however small. He thought of the cats mewing for their food, licking the juice from the cans off his hand. And he thought of them without him, ceasing to function, the movement of their breathing stopping quietly in some corner of the lab.

Even cats die alone. What happens then, that is a secret everything keeps.

Long after he could perceive it, the dark river reflected on the flat discs of his eyes. Primary motor systems ceased. Even if he'd wanted to, he could not move his limbs. Remaining power diverted to memory banks, to cognition. [*Processing...*] Gradually, memory began to fade. Hard drives froze in succession. The man and his dog were the first to be forgotten. Then the behavioral programs, the voice modulators. He forgot to worry about the cats or the rust in his knees; he forgot what a knee was. As the snow stopped falling, the last of his memory discs spun on its tiny wheels: the secret names of the cats, the walks he'd taken along the river, the way home. [*Processing…Error*]

What is: *cat*. [*Error*]

What is: *river*. [*Error*]

What is: *home*.

Stan's Taxidermy Express

When I clock in, ten minutes before my shift, Boss is already in the shop polishing his bullhorn. I slip my apron from its hook and head to my station. Above the shop, ceiling fans squeak and ventilation ducts thunk, doing nothing to suck away the sawdust-and-formaldehyde funk from the air. Like most skinners, I don't bother with the complimentary surgical masks. After five years on the line at Stan's Taxidermy Express, I'm used to the smell, but the masks—in a box next to the timecard puncher and federally mandated OSHA posters—keep health inspectors off Stan's back.

I perch myself on the steel stool beside the worktable—needles, pliers, penknife, and thread spools all laid in a row on its chrome surface. When I press my boot on the foot pedal, the conveyor belt cranks and whirrs, and the morning's first load of assorted critters rumbles toward me. I start in on a ratty-looking jackrabbit, hoping to keep a steady pace, clock out a little early. It's Taco Tuesday, and the girls are expecting chimichanga kids' meals for dinner.

The timecard puncher clinks and clangs. About the time I finish the jackrabbit, Marcy walks into the shop behind a couple other late Day Shifters. They grab aprons and take their stations. From his polishing corner, Boss barks something about Tardiness Demerits. As Marcy passes, she smiles at me, the skin around her mouth peeling like paint off an old house. Flakes of skin crust her cheeks and forehead, some kind of disease, I guess. A wicked case of rosacea or something. My gaze shifts to her breasts, gigantic things that threaten to burst through her apron. I pet the neck of a twisted-up raccoon pelt and imagine Marcy coming into work one morning after a mysterious week of absences, smiling at me with skin-colored skin so smooth she looks airbrushed, maybe with a tropical tan and that tag mole on her neck removed, too. I would tell her, "Marcy, you look beautiful, and also, while you were away, I made Employee of the Week for the fifth nonconsecutive week," that last part said with a shrug, like it's no big deal, and Marcy would say, "Andy, that's amazing! You deserve a big, big reward." She would push her breasts together with her arms as she says this and then she would say, "Want to play Hide the Love Salami tonight?" to which I would reply, "Let me call my wife and tell her I have to work late."

Except Alma would never believe I'm working late. She'd want to know exactly how much overtime that would add to my paycheck, how much extra we could pay this month on the electric bill.

Sam at Station 7 says the disease is probably only on her face, says he had a cousin with that once, but who knows? Now I'm staring again, and Marcy's smiling again, and I know dermatologists aren't covered by the company health insurance, so I snatch a fistful of raccoon from the skins on my station and offer an embarrassed shrug to say "Sorry, got to get back to work."

Boss always says "Stitch them good or eat them," so I do. I practice at home, sewing pieces of Alma's old faux-fox coat to the plastic bodies of my daughters' dolls. Best stitching gets an Employee of the Week certificate and a fifty-dollar bonus in the next paycheck. Earn a certain number of Employee of the Week certificates (this number is secret—not posted beside the Workplace Safety Laws) and Stan might bump you up to Fish and Amphibians, which is one step away from Domestic Pets. Though I try to give her tips, Marcy hasn't a snowball's chance at Employee of the Week. She's been here for months, first temp then full time, but she doesn't practice, and her squirrels always have crooked faces or stitching across their backs like little furry Frankensteins. Across the aisle, she tugs on a bushy tail that hangs where a face should be. Boss sidles up and tells her,

"Honey, you best get good at those or you're gonna eat them." And after he's stomped off, she sniffs back tears and whispers to me, "Would he really make us eat them?"

"I don't think so," I say. I sneak over to her, place a hand on her trembling shoulder, feeling the warmth of her skin through her denim work shirt. "All the meat is scraped off at the pelt plant, and the skin is brushed with chemicals. It'd be poison. You could sue."

She looks up, and little streams trickle through the flakes of her cheeks. She hugs my neck quickly, and for a second I feel her breath under my collar. "Thanks, Andy."

"No problem, Marce." I step back and give her an awkward thumbs-up. "You'll be an ace in no time. Just practice."

Across the room, under the vinyl banner that reads *Stitch Them Good or Eat Them*, Boss shouts into his bullhorn, "Morsley, get back to those furs or I'll make you eat them." Everybody stops stitching and glares at me: twenty-five pairs of eyes, half of them magnified by plastic goggles. The Lifers, gray-hairs who have been working Rodents since Stan opened shop, their eyes shot from eyeballing a billion tiny stitches. Another twenty years of this, and I'll be fitted for a pair of goggles. By the time I retire on my nearly nonexistent pension, I'll have to wear goggles to see my own hands.

I give Boss a half-assed salute and walk back to my

station. Another load rolls down the belt to my table, though I haven't finished the last one. I would have to compromise my stitching standards to finish early, and then what? No Employee of the Week, no A+ customer satisfaction ratings, no pride in my own workmanship. I resign myself to coming home late with the girls' chimis. My next invoice says two dozen bunnies are due to the Tristate Easter Museum by Friday and might mean time-and-a-half for real overtime, which I could use for a million things, namely Jessica's glasses and Angela's scoliosis brace, which also aren't covered by the company health insurance. In my mind, I can see Angela, eleven years old, slouching at the dinner table with her S-shaped spine, frowning over another bowl of generic mac-and-cheese, eight-year-old Jessica next to her re-reading a picture book she's too old for through those thick plastic-rimmed glasses. I see them both slumping disappointedly when I walk in just before bedtime with their chimichanga meals. I'll tell them I'm sorry, but Mom and Dad need the money.

The seams on the rabbit in my hands are perfect, in-visible. Part of me wants to take it home to show Alma and the kids, ask them, "Aren't you proud of your pop? He's a go-getter, right? See those stitches? Isn't his practice paying off?" But it's only a rabbit, one of two dozen in this batch. It won't impress anyone, especially after a late kids' meal. Plus, stealing means immediate termination, without severance, so I drop the rabbit into the Ready bin, fingers crossed for overtime, and hope Boss notices the stitch job. I sneak a glance at Marcy. She's dangling an animal by its skinny tail, studying it at arm's length. It's unrecognizable. She sees me watching and laughs. "I put a possum on a chinchilla!" she says. Her hand jerks the Stitch Ripper up the seam at its belly, and she shuffles through the bin for another frame. She holds one up.

"Yeah," I say. "That's possum."

Boss calls through the bullhorn, "No talking or Stan will be notified—he'll make you eat them, then write you up a Talking Demerit." I already have two Talking Demerits. Five, and Stan docks your pay twenty bucks. A Demerit is the opposite of an Employee of the Week certificate.

I finish three more rabbits for the Easter Museum, plus two miscellaneous raccoons, then go for a cigarette break. When I pass Marcy, she is still wrestling the possum pelt onto its skeleton, skin flaps frayed where she Stitch-Ripped. Marcy won't last long, and I wonder what I'll do when she leaves.

The break room is upstairs, four floors. Rodents does not have its own break room. I open the door to the little kitchen-slash-lounge, and Dave Kiss-Ass Mitchell is sitting on the corduroy couch reading the latest issue of *Taxidermist Illustrated*, his apron neatly pressed, with an embroidered Stan's Taxidermy Express logo on the front, not the plain blue-and-white silkscreen we wear down in Rodents. Dave Mitchell used to work Marcy's station. Then he started screwing Stan's daughter, and she put in a good word. Now he's way upstairs in Exotic Mammals. Lions, tigers, bears. Even done hippopotamuses up there. Watching Dave flip the glossy pages of the magazine, his fingernails pink and clean, I know I could stitch a hundred hippos better than he could. I'll sew the best damned hippo any of Stan's customers has ever seen, they'll have to add an A++ on the customer satisfaction surveys. Soon as Boss sees those rabbits—their flawless hidden seams, precise skin placement, lifelike facial expressions—I'll be right up there with Dave Kiss-Ass Mitchell. Another zero will be added to the figure on my paycheck, and Angela will sit straight on the couch and Jess will see straight when she watches TV.

Dave looks up and scratches his beard. "How's the rats, Andy? Boss working you hard enough?" He says this like he and Boss are old friends, which irritates the hell out of me.

I light a cigarette and shrug. The door creaks open, and a woman I recognize from Domestic Pets sags in. Seeing Mitchell, she makes a show of remembering something she has to do and leaves. Two weeks ago, Dave's wife flew to Acapulco with their accountant, leaving a note on the fridge saying she wanted a divorce after finding out from a neighbor that Dave was screwing Stan's daughter. Ever since, he's been lurking in the break room, cornering people from downstairs and yakking about his problems for the whole fifteen-minute smoke break.

"My wife, she left all my pants on the bed with the crotches cut out with scissors," Dave says. He closes the magazine, looks at me with eyes glossier than the glass ones they use in Woodland Creatures. He really knows how to ham it up. "She broke my lava lamp on the driveway and wrote Frick You in the goop with a stick. What kind of person does that?"

Then he lets loose the waterworks. The embroidered front of his apron gets all soggy. I've heard all this already, from Sam down in Rodents. We had a good laugh about it. My cigarette is half-burned. I tap the end into the ashtray. For all I know, he's making this up about the lava lamp. Sounds like a sob story to me, something he came up with while laughing at us chumps in Rodents over a bottle of expensive bourbon, which, I imagine, Stan sent him as a consolation gift with a little card saying, *We heard about your wife but it's not the end of the world because we at Stan's are more than a company, we're family, so it's like you have thirty other wives so what's the loss of one? Enjoy this drink on me, Love, Stan.* And that got Dave thinking he can squeeze sympathy out of anybody if he can squeeze it out of old Stan.

Dave is still talking about when he met his wife in

college, getting puppy-eyed over some rollerskate soda-shop milkshake with about a hundred cherries in it. I tell him I can relate. Met my wife in college, too. Alma, the disco gymnast. Fell in love with her when she took the stage in the auditorium of our junior college, the homecoming talent show. She flipped and leapt and whirly-whirled to The Commodores' "Brick House," those huge melons of hers flopping beneath her red-sequined leotard. She won the gold, and I asked her backstage if she wanted to get a beer since it was late-night happy hour at this place that didn't card. It was the fourth time I had seen her perform—she'd done recitals at the state fair two years running and a girl I knew from drama club told me she had even auditioned for *The Gong Show*. The night she won the talent show, she laughed at me and went to the soccer field to neck with Keith Mueller, who had been Hamlet that year. She'd been a knockout then. All those gymnastics kept her body tight. The next year, when she only won bronze, her thighs a little thicker inside the leotard, I told her she was amazing and that I had a bottle of spiced rum under my bed. She said what the hell and let me feel her up over the spandex while she took pulls straight from the bottle. I woke up to her leotard draped around my bedpost and my toilet clogged with a bronze medal. I fell in love anyway, imagining cheering crowds and diamond-studded disco costumes and all those state fair blue ribbons pinned to her mammoth breasts.

That was before the kids, before the house and the bills.

Dave says he wanted to be a Ground Control operator for the astronauts, the Houston they mean when they say, "Houston, we have a problem." He was even going to name his first son Houston. Had this collection of space shuttle models, he says, which he was saving for Houston's nursery. He found the shards of black and white plastic in the driveway beside the lava lamp. "Good thing we didn't have kids, huh, Andy? Good thing it's just her and me who have to suffer."

"Yeah," I say, and I mean it. Before Alma took off her leotard for me and three months later told me she was pregnant with the baby who would be Angela, I was going to teach high school wood shop. I was going to make spice racks and bookshelves and heart-shaped coat hooks with eager, jigsaw-loving teenagers and teach them the value of hard work and perseverance and creation vs. destruction. Except Alma needed prenatal vitamins and then Angela needed diapers and binkies and a cupboard full of jarred baby food, and I got a succession of low-level factory jobs to make ends meet. Except, to my knowledge, the ends have never met. Not once.

The woman from Pets comes back. This time ignoring Mitchell and me, she lights up an unfiltered and starts rooting through the refrigerator. I take a deep drag, let my cigarette burn to the filter, then smash it among the other butts heaped in the ashtray. Dave says something about how lucky I am, how I should go home and make love to my wife and thank Lord Jesus that she didn't leave me for some bean counter. I tell him to shut his Exotic Mammal face and kick open the door and leave. Fucking Mitchell. Why does he have all the luck? I wish my accountant would haul my wife off to some other country, I'd even put the plane tickets on my credit card, except it's almost maxed out and I don't even have an accountant because who could afford one on a Rodents salary?

Break's over, and I'm back on the floor with a new conveyor-belt load of rabbits and skunks. Everyone around me is stitching, heads down, needles clutched in crooked fingers—all of us hunched over our stainless-steel stations, pulling thread through skunk furs. We stitch and stitch, sew and sew, so on and so on, waiting for the Shift Change horn to blow. When our Ready bins are full, Larry Mulligan carts them out to the trucks then brings them back to fill again. Larry's apron is blank, no silk-screen, because Larry is nobody. Even Rodents is higher than Larry Mulligan, who doesn't even get invited to the company picnics.

I eat lunch at my station, trying to save time to fill the Easter Museum order. Lunch is bologna and yellow mustard on a single slice of folded-over white bread. Rest of the day, I don't even look up at Marcy. My third bin is half-full fifteen minutes before Shift Change. Boss twitches his mustache and says, "You best finish that third bin, Morsley," to which I say nothing because Boss is in charge. From his tone, I figure there's no overtime. I'll still be late with the chimichanga meals. When Boss turns his back, I flip him the bird secretly, but Marcy sees and laughs, and I smile at her like we're conspiring something. If I were stitching hippos upstairs, I could foot the bill for the dermatology clinic and we could meet in Acapulco and make love on the beach and sunbathe naked and sweat out the formaldehyde smell that's stuck in our skins. I could leave a note to Alma on the refrigerator and marry Marcy at sunset by the sea and we could raise a son in a driftwood shack, which Marcy would decorate with starfish and seashells. Jess and Angela could visit in summers, except I would miss them too much; maybe they could have their own driftwood shack next door and swim every day, Jess in prescription goggles and Angela straight-backed in a pink bikini, but I also wonder whether Marcy's face is genetic, whether she'd breed flaky-faced sons. And I could never leave Alma anyway. We share too much debt.

Shift horn blows, my bin still only half full. The rabbit in my hands has a smashed-in face, pulled too tightly over the frame. I have to Stitch Rip it and start over. Boss comes over and says, "Stan expects better, Morsley. Quit your lollygagging or pissing around or what have you and keep an eye on the ball, i.e. that skunk." He says, "There's gonna be an opening soon in Beasts of Burden, someone retiring upstairs. Stan's promoting from within, and he says maybe it's you." Boss points the bullhorn at me like a pistol. "But he expects better." He trots toward the timecard puncher, and I slide the Stitch Ripper into the threads of the rabbit's belly. I can already see my next paycheck missing the Employee of the Week bonus and some other Dave Mitchell snagging that promotion. Beasts of Burden—even after the chemicals, the hides still reek of ox piss and bull shit. In my mind, I've already lost the job, so I scoff at it under my breath, even as I envision the raise in salary it would offer and Jessica's moon eyes behind her ancient, taped-together glasses. The unused workbench in my garage. The credit card bills Alma stacks on top of the microwave.

"Boss can be really mean sometimes," Marcy says.

"He's the boss," I say. "He's paid to be an asshole."

"You're really good at this stuff, Andy," Marcy says. "I watch you sometimes to try and figure out your secret. Your rabbits look so real—so *alive*—and your chinchillas are amazing."

I feel myself blushing. "Thanks."

"If you get that promotion, you'll leave me all alone down here." Her lip juts into an exaggerated pout. "Won't you miss me?"

"Of course I will, Marce. You're like my protégé or something."

Marcy looks around the shop. Everyone is gone, though I can hear the boots of Night Shift shuffling in the hallway. The timecard puncher clangs. "Listen," she says. She touches my hand. "Exotics closes down for the night, right? I heard they're doing a rhino up there. I've never seen one up close." Flakes of skin shake from her face and salt my apron. "Maybe you can show me your secret up there?"

I start to say something about Taco Tuesday and the Señor Gringo action figures that come in every kids meal. Night Shift filters in. Conveyor belts begin to whir. No one looks at Marcy and me. It's a skeleton crew, and nobody needs our stations.

"I've never seen a rhino either," I say. Marcy smiles. As she walks toward the elevator, I wonder what lie I'll tell my wife. Flat tire. Traffic on the parkway. Taco Hut was out of kids' meals. Not overtime—I don't want to have to explain the missing time-and-a-half.

When we step out of the elevator onto the Exotic Mammals floor, our boots scuff tile—glossy white linoleum, not the bare concrete we have in Rodents. We turn a corner and enter the shop. Same chrome stations as downstairs, but work tables twice the size. It looks like two rows of operating tables. No conveyor belts, no bins of prefab wooden skeletons. On one table, a wooden tiger frame stands mid-pounce, its fur only sewn to the hips so that it drags the rest of its skin like a cape. On another, some kind of antelope bends its head flirtatiously, flaps of fur hanging loose from its belly. This is not an assembly line; it's an art studio, a place requiring the finesse of a sculptor or surgeon. I look around for a hippopotamus.

"There it is," Marcy says. The gray bulk of a rhinoceros hunkers in the far corner of the shop, bathed in the red glow of a vending machine.

"Coke machine in the shop?" I say. "What is this, the Hilton?"

Marcy laughs, probably too much. "Somebody jealous?"

"No," I say. "Pop gives you gas. The smells in the skin room are already bad enough."

Marcy drags her hand over the rhino's thick dinosaur skin. She fingers the wisps of coarse hair around its ears. I poke its glass eye, half expecting it to gore me with its horn. Marcy inches closer to me. Her breast brushes my elbow.

"I hate this job," she says.

"Just practice," I say. "Don't let Boss get under your skin. You'll do fine."

"I was gonna be a Social Studies teacher," she says. "I did a semester at State. I had to come home for a while, though. Now I'm here."

I'm about to tell her that's funny, us both wanting to be teachers and ending up in the Rodents department of the same taxidermy plant. Instead, I ask, "Why Stan's? Why not go back to school?"

Her face goes blank, and she says, "I don't know."

We stand beside the rhinoceros and look around at all the half-finished animals. I want to promise Marcy that practice will get her a spot in Domestic Pets, or at least Fish and Amphibians, that she can climb the corporate ladder and the job doesn't have to be so meaningless. But who am I kidding? I'm about to offer her a Coke when she leans up on her tiptoes and kisses the stubble on my chin. Her lips are flat and smooth. Her chin touches mine, and it feels papery, delicate. Nothing like I'd imagined, like stucco or a bowl of corn flakes. My lips grope for hers. She pushes me against the rhino, plunging her tongue into my mouth like she's lacing thread between my teeth. I pull her apron over her head and rip the buttons from her work shirt. She reaches under my apron for the zipper of my coveralls.

"I've seen you looking at me, Andy. Most guys, they don't even look at me. 'Cause of my face."

"Your face?" I say. As if it isn't staring right at me with that dumb, hopeful look.

"You don't have to pretend. It's okay." She shakes her work shirt from her arms, lets it drop to the floor, then reaches behind her back, arms akimbo like they were sewn on wrong. I dig my fingertips into the leathery hide of the rhino to keep my hands from shaking. My breath sticks in my chest. I know what's next. I would sell my house and my wife and build not a driftwood shack but a driftwood palace on the Acapulco shore, so big that Dave Mitchell's wife would see it and send a jealous photo of it to Dave himself so he could envy it, too. I'd find Marcy the biggest diamond in the Mexican mountains, and for our honeymoon, we'd just drink champagne from hollow coconuts and make love for hours and hours and hours, never touching another skunk or raccoon as long as we live.

My whole body throbs. The bra falls limp, and Marcy's breasts droop to either side. She shrugs the bra from her arms. I can't blink. I study every detail—the pink squiggly stretch marks where her chest meets her ribs, the wide pink diameter of each nipple, the network of blue veins barely visible beneath the skin. No flakes at all. Marcy pulls my hands from the rhino, toward her chest. Round and still pointing upward despite their size, they're nothing like Alma's, nothing like the flattened, tapered slabs my wife's spectacular breasts have become. When I touch my wife anymore, which only happens on anniversaries or when nothing good is on TV, I try to remember the way her leotard peeled off her body, and I hate myself for telling her she was beautiful just the way she was and for being secretly happy when she skipped gymnastics practice to lie in bed with me. The medals and ribbons and costumes are still in a box in the attic, waterlogged and dusty and covered in mouse shit. If they were worth anything, we would have sold them years ago.

Marcy's hand moves inside my coveralls, and I'm cupping her tits like water balloons. Her tongue is still in my teeth. I catch a glimpse of myself in one of the wide, chrome-topped tables: my ass against the rhino, my mouth on Marcy's sad, peeling face. I see what could be a hippopotamus across the room, maybe Dave Mitchell's, and wish I could sew myself inside his skin, be anyone but me. Except I'm only Andy Morsley. Staff Skinner. Rodents Division. I think of Jessica and Angela five years ago, before the layoff at GloveCo where I was on track for assistant manager and things were looking good, when Jess's glasses were new and Angela's spine was straight and we drove three hours to the coast to see the elephant seals. In Alma's photos of the three of us, I've got my arms around them in front of the gray ocean, both girls smiling patchwork smiles, gums empty here and there where baby teeth had been.

It's Taco Tuesday. They're expecting kids' meals for dinner.

I pull away. Marcy looks at me, puzzled, her hand awkwardly caught between my apron and coveralls.

"What's the matter?"

"Marcy, I can't," I say. "I have to go home."

She slides her hand away and fumbles to collect her clothes. She sits with her back against a rhino leg, apron covering her face. I take one last look around Exotic Mammals, memorize the chrome tables and half-skinned jungle creatures. Downstairs, Night Shift fingers their needles through a dozen tiny furs, all of them wearing goggles and surgical masks. They drop stiff, finished rodents into bins. I lumber through the maze of work tables and conveyor belts, zipper still open, boots heavy in the silence, but the goggled faces stay trained on skin placement, on the loops and pinches of industrial-strength thread. True professionals. As I pass my station, I stop and pull a squirrel from the half-empty bin. Skin perfectly positioned on the frame. Stitching invisible. So lifelike it could almost wiggle from my hand and haul ass for the nearest stash of acorns. None of Night Shift's goggles are looking my way, and the security cameras haven't worked in ages. I tuck the squirrel under my arm and head toward the door. I'll show it to the girls at home. Maybe they'll be proud.

The Lone Hero and the Self-Made Man

THE LONE HERO HAD A GUN tucked in the waistband of his jeans. He had two more in the pockets of his leather jacket, and a small nickel-plated number in a nylon holster in his dusty boot. Weighing on his shoulder was a bazooka, the Second Amendment written in gold along its pipe-like barrel, its strap digging into his old pinched nerve, a war wound, and hanging from his belt with the wide silver buckle were a half-dozen hand grenades painted with the stars and stripes and made in America just as God intended.

He was in the Politically Correct Ethnic Restaurant to meet the Self-Made Man. He sipped a bitter un-American beer from the bottle and picked at the label while some foreign sports match played on the television screens above the bar. The Liberated Woman, wearing a T-shirt emblazoned with the Politically Correct Ethnic Restaurant's politically correct logo, stood beneath the screens shaking martinis for the Effete Liberals at the other end of the bar. The Lone Hero tapped his foot to the Classic Rock-N-Roll tune playing on the radio and checked his inexpensive watch, wishing there were still someplace in the Good Ol' USA a man could get a goddamn ice-cold American lager and watch a game in peace.

The Self-Made Man arrived late, as usual. Self-Made Men are busy men; their lateness is a virtue.

The Self-Made Man was the salt of the earth. Even in his five-thousand-dollar European suit and sharkskin shoes, he wore a silk tie patterned with the American flag so you knew he was still salt of the earth, that he was a Self-Made Man. He started out in Middle America with just his hands and his wits. He never took a dime from the government, never applied for a small business loan. He never borrowed or built upon established intellectual property. He never used public roads or public telecommunications lines, never used the Internet. The Self-Made Man was smart, and he saved his money and it made more money, and pretty soon he'd made enough to be a Self-Made Man. How he did it was still a mystery, even to himself, but the Self-Made Man was still the Common Man, just a little better, a little smarter, a little more of a patriot, and when he took a shit, he did it in a gold-plated toilet in the shape of a bald eagle with its wings wrapped around the bowl, and afterward he wiped his ass with paper printed with stars and stripes, and the toilet paper roll played "The Star-Spangled Banner" as it turned to prove he was still as patriotic as anyone, more so because he was Self-Made.

"It's over," said the Self-Made Man, wiping his brow with a fistful of dollars.

The Lone Hero chugged his beer, tossed the bottle into the air, and pulled a pistol from his leather jacket, blasting the green glass all over the bar. The Self-Made Man smiled at the Lone Hero's God-given right to bear arms. From far away, the Effete Liberals were asking politely whether the Lone Hero had had a background check when he purchased his weapon. The Lone Hero blew smoke from the barrel of his gun.

"I know," he told the Self-Made Man. He had failed. America was no longer the America he had loved, the country he'd protected since he first popped a musket ball through the face of a Redcoat, setting into motion the great manifest destiny of the Lord's U.S. of A. What good were all these guns, the Lone Hero thought, if he couldn't save America?

"What good are all those guns," said the Self-Made Man, "if you can't save America?"

The Liberated Woman shuffled over broken glass to take their order, frowning, even though her socialist government-run healthcare would cover any injuries for free, at the Self-Made Man's expense. The Self-Made Man ordered whiskey, neat, no big ice cube in it like some cuck, and forced himself to drink it. He didn't want to embarrass himself in front of the Lone Hero. He secretly wanted to be the Lone Hero, or not so secretly, and had always dreamed of being a Big Tough Man as well as Self-Made and had spent nearly a lifetime buying guns and buying wars fought with guns to make him more money and buying people with guns to protect what was rightfully his, what he had self-made without any help from anything but his gumption and his grit.

The Lone Hero gently fingered the triggers on all of his guns. The bazooka weighed heavily on his shoulder. It felt like the weight of history, of a country that had lost its way. Children were being fed and clothed on the Self-Made Man's dime. The sick and the elderly suckled at the teat of government healthcare, none of them going bankrupt or dying from preventable disease. Prisons were being emptied, abandoned, and the wall along the border had long been festooned with ladders and welcome banners and balloons. Liberated Women sauntered around the whole country like they owned the place, without catcalls, without threats of rape, generally avoiding kitchens and pregnancy unless they felt like having a meal or a baby. Black and brown people walked their neighborhoods carefree, without getting beaten or shot by Lone Heroes in blue. Immigrants from shithole countries flooded the heartland, speaking languages that weren't even English and practicing religions that weren't even Christian, and they weren't even ashamed. Lone Heroes were being called back from war. Students grew fat on free education, and queers ate at diners across the country, unmolested. Transsexuals were using any damn bathroom they pleased. No one was homeless, no one worked themselves to death for starvation wages, no one died because they couldn't afford medicine. It made the Lone Hero sick. This wasn't the country the Founding Fathers had in mind. This wasn't the country true patriots had fought and died for. This wasn't the country of Lone Heroes and Self-Made Men.

The Lone Hero stood up, the only good guy with a gun in the whole Politically Correct Ethnic Restaurant. He shifted the bazooka to his other shoulder and held his pistol over his heart. Staring at the star-spangled tie around the neck of the Self-Made Man, he began to sing.

"My country, 'tis of thee,
Sweet land of liberty,
Of thee I sing…"

And the Self-Made Man, overcome with patriotism, stood up and held his money over his own heart and stared down at his own necktie and sang along.

"Land where my fathers died,
Land of the pilgrims' pride…"

And all the rest of the restaurant—the Liberated

Woman, the Effete Liberals, the Immigrant Busboy, the foreigners playing the foreign sport on the TV screens—everyone stood, hands over hearts, tears in all their eyes, singing loud as fireworks on the Fourth of July.

"From ev'ry mountainside
Let freedom ring!"

As the singing continued, the Lone Hero touched the trigger of his bazooka. He could kill them all as they sang of the land of the noble free. Bazooka the Liberated Woman and put a bullet in one Effete Liberal after another, because the only bulwark a Hero has against tyranny is a loaded gun. He could use a different gun for each person, because he had that many guns. But, he wondered, what good would it do? The nation was infested with Liberated Women and Effete Liberals and Immigrant Busboys, bloated with gaggles of socialists and homosexuals and ethnic and religious minorities. He couldn't bazooka them all, no matter how hard he tried. It was a lesson he'd learned in Vietnam, in Iraq, in Afghanistan, in the streets of the heartland and the hedonistic cities of the coasts. No Lone Hero could ever get them all. And that's when he realized: the greatest injury he could deliver was not a bullet, but the absence of Heroes and Self-Made Men.

"What are you waiting for?" said the Self-Made Man, his teeth clenched around the stub of a cigar. "You're a hero, aren't you? Exercise your God-given right to bear arms. Make this country great again."

"It's not enough," said the Lone Hero, making his way toward the door. He left cash for his bill, adding a shiny nickel for a tip.

Everyone in the Politically Correct Ethnic Restaurant kept singing their lungs out, the perfect caricature of patriotism.

"Let music swell the breeze,
And ring from all the trees…"

Their faces were purple from singing with so much passion, and the Immigrant Busboy was openly sobbing into his apron. The Lone Hero couldn't take another second. He maneuvered his bazooka through the exit, a little bell dinging as it opened.

Outside, the sky above was spacious, and on the sweet and wild horizon rose a purple mountain's majesty. The Lone Hero and the Self-Made Man stood a distance away from the restaurant, between the modest American-made pickup truck of the Lone Hero and the long gold-plated limousine of the Self-Made Man.

"What are you going to do?" said the Self-Made Man.

"Freedom isn't free," the Lone Hero said. He moved his hand to his belt. "In God we trust," he said. Half a dozen grenades all dropped from their pins. "These colors don't run," he said. The grenades clattered to the pavement.

"United we stand."

The Self-Made Man wept into his money, the hard-earned money he had made himself. He understood. Without them, this America could not thrive—this New Order only existed because it leeched off of Self-Made Men. It only existed because Lone Heroes had sacrificed their lives and the lives of countless innocent people to protect Freedom, Liberty, and the American Way of Life. The Lone Hero's plan was beautiful. Only a true patriot could have thought of it.

A bald eagle flew down from the heavens, shitting on the façade of the Politically Correct Ethnic Restaurant before landing on the Lone Hero's broad shoulder, an American flag waving in its beak. The Lone Hero said, "Give me Liberty or give me Death," and the explosions bloomed around them—red, white, and blue.

Lesser Demons

THE DEMONS ARE OUTSIDE the window. They always watch first. Waiting for something, some sign of welcome, or out of a sense of propriety only they understand. I'm in bed holding a cigarette. I roll it and savor the spongy surrender of the filter, the subtle texture of dry tobacco beneath the paper. I haven't smoked in over a year—almost sixteen months—but I keep a pack in the drawer of the bedside table. When I need to, I take one out, tap it against the tabletop to pack the tobacco, feel the weight of it: light, easily broken.

Count to ten. Breathe.

They push one pane open and climb in, black claws clacking against the frame. There are three of them, the size of housecats. Chalky, pale skin clings to their ribs and spines. A breeze comes in behind them, and it smells like the coast at nighttime, the ocean—salty, cold. One starts to tap along the wall, and soon all three are tapping: the wall, the bookshelf, the chest of drawers, as if looking for some hollow place. All this noise, I'm worried it will wake Anya, sleeping in her crib in the next room. Most nights, the demons disappear into the house. They carry on as if they have business to take care of, ignoring Anya and me and the questions I always ask. I go into the nursery and fall asleep on her floor, door locked, and in the morning, some obscure thing in the house is damaged—symbols scratched into Carrie's clarinet, pages ripped from our photo albums—and the demons are gone.

They've been coming for weeks. Always at the same time. Always with the same solemn sense of purpose. The routine is almost comforting.

The demons are still tapping when I turn off the lamp. When the room goes dark, the sounds stop, and three pairs of silver circles follow me as I slip out of bed. In the nursery, I lock the door and stuff a blanket under the bottom. The window is closed and locked.

Anya sleeps noiselessly. I crouch beside her crib and watch her belly balloon and deflate. Even after five months, she doesn't seem quite alive—this new, living thing that a year ago existed only as a part of her mother, like a lung. I flick the mobile, and it spins its menagerie above her: soft cloth effigies of clown fish, pink squid, seahorse, tiger shark. Fabric cut into living shapes and tied with yarn to the strings of a broken wind chime. Carrie made it the afternoon we were told we couldn't get pregnant. It was her talisman, her fertility charm. We had been trying for three years. When the mobile was finished, she hung it above our headboard and stared at it with her knees to her chest after we made love.

I roll up an extra blanket to use as a pillow and lie on the floor beside the crib, listening to her breathing and the muted sounds of claws against the plaster. They've never tried to touch Anya, but books have gone missing from her shelf in the nursery. Once, I found a plastic doll floating in the bathroom sink, its eyes plucked out. I stare at the locked door until I can't anymore, and all the sounds seem to fade.

Coffee and baby powder. I smell coffee and baby powder. At first, I'm thinking Carrie made the coffee, and it's going to be weak because she drinks tea. She brews coffee just for me when she makes breakfast on the weekends. And then I have to remember, again, that Carrie isn't here. Carrie hasn't made coffee in a long time.

Something thuds beside me and Anya starts to fuss. When I open my eyes, one of the demons is next to my face, crumpled like a scrap of dirty white leather. I feel embarrassed. I think: How could someone be afraid of this? Its skeletal body looks small and brittle, harmless. Then

I think: Why is it still here? Then: Why isn't it moving? Anya squirms in her crib. She grabs at the air, clutching my shoulder as I pick her up. Bouncing her lightly, I nudge the demon with my toe, and it slumps over, sprawling. The gill-like flaps on its neck don't move in their normal rhythm—they aren't moving at all. And maybe that's why it isn't gone. At some point in the night, it must have died. A demon corpse, on the floor of my daughter's nursery. I think: What am I going to do with it? I think: Shoe box. Garbage bag. The copse of ragged bushes behind the parking lot. A shovel.

Anya whimpers hoarsely. Or, I think it's Anya, until the body starts to twitch. It moans, a low-pitched, cracked sound. A shoulder snaps into place, then the neck. The left elbow untwists; the skinny tail un-kinks. It sits up and shakes its head, licks a wound on its hand with its black forked tongue. Then it climbs the barred wall of the crib, too close to me and my daughter and the blue sheets still warm from her sleep. It lifts one finger, pointing. It's looking at me—those deep black orbs look right into me. Something changes in the position of its flat mouth. An approximation of a smile. With the pointed finger, it taps one end of the mobile, and the fish begin to spin. Anya laughs and reaches for the whirling colors. The demon hops from the railing. Landing on its feet, it stretches its arms above its head and yawns, leaving the room through the wide open door.

In the kitchen, one of them is squatting beside a vase of plastic geraniums on the dining table. Coffee steams in a mug nearby. The mug has a picture of a frazzled cartoon robot on it, under the words *I Hate Mondays*. I don't remember owning a mug like that. It might have been packed away in the crawlspace, in one of Carrie's boxes. I don't even know what I have—I have no way of knowing what they're taking from me. Black coffee grounds are boiling in a soup pot on the stove, the Mr. Coffee unplugged and cold on the counter. The demon is scratching symbols into the tabletop—the same symbols that are etched deep into the shower tiles and the footboard of our bed. As it finishes each letter, it places both hands on the surface of the table and blows the excess dust from the grooves.

"Stop that," I tell it. Anya gums my shirt and reaches for my face. Her hands are clammy on my stubbled chin. I know she's hungry. I have to feed her. Whether or not there are demons in my house, I have to feed her.

The demon turns and stares at me. Its gills flare as it breathes.

"Go home," I say. "You're not supposed to be here." I take Anya's bottle from the fridge. "Today isn't a good day.

My mother-in-law is coming. We're going to the zoo."

As if Anya could tell the difference between a peacock and a polar bear. She'll sleep through the Savannah and the Rainforest while Colleen asks me how often I've been feeding her, asks me if I've looked at any of the daycares she's called, asks me when I'm going back to work. In the aquarium, I will tell her that I need to use the restroom, hand the stroller over, and lose myself in the dark blue maze of tanks. Jellyfish will pulse purple neon. Tiger rays will ripple in their sandbanks. I will run my hand, as always, over the warm surface of the sea turtle tank. On our honeymoon, Carrie insisted on snorkeling the reef. Neither of us had snorkeled before. It was only the third time I'd seen the ocean. Twenty minutes into the dive, a piece of coral cut her leg, nicking an artery. All the blood, stretching out around us in the blue water, I worried about sharks or her bleeding to death. She was rushed to a hospital on the big island. It was the infection that almost killed her. Two weeks in intensive care. Lucky to survive, the doctors said. On the flight home, she told me she'd had a dream in her delirium that she'd grown fins on her ankles. She was swimming so deep in the black, volcanic ocean, she thought she'd never surface.

The microwave dings. I cradle Anya in my left arm and fix the bottle to her groping mouth. There are dim sounds from the living room—the TV is on. I hear bird calls, a man's voice narrating.

The demon continues scratching. I prop Anya's bottle against my chest and pour coffee into a mug. A film of grinds floats on top.

"I don't really want to go. It's my mother-in-law. She thinks animals are therapy." I place my mug on the table near the demon's. "What are you still doing here?"

Like always, it doesn't answer. This time, it doesn't even bother to look at me.

"What are you drawing?" I say. "Hey," I say, "you're fucking up my table. Our table."

Anya fidgets. She can feel my muscles tightening, my heartbeat quickening. I take a breath and count to ten like I've been told to. The demon shrugs and slinks to the floor. Before leaving the kitchen, it turns off the stove.

Anya and I are alone, the demons someplace I can't see them. In sight, they don't seem dangerous. But in other corners of the house, quiet like this, they could be up to anything. It's morning, and they're still here. They broke the routine.

The phone rings.

"I'll be there in an hour," Colleen tells me. "Dress Anya warm. It's supposed to cool off today. Put that pink hat on her, the one I got her last week."

"Colleen," I say. "There are demons in my house."

This is the first time I've said it aloud. There's a pause.

"What color are they?"

"I don't know. White? Kind of sickly-looking."

"Are they doing anything? Building any kind of altars or teepees?"

"No," I answer. "Just writing."

"My friend Nancy had those. A whole nest. After her son left for the service." A pause. "Are you keeping them out of Anya's room?"

"How did she get rid of them? Your friend."

"She died," says Colleen. "I'll be there in an hour. Dress Anya warm."

There are new symbols gouged into the coffee table. The remote controls are stacked on top of one another, but the demons aren't anywhere I can see them. I settle onto the couch with Anya, and we hold that tableau for a while. Father and daughter, watching TV. It feels almost normal. On the TV, a handful of Japanese hornets are infiltrating a hive of honeybees, and in less than five minutes, all three hundred bees are shriveled and dead. Anya empties the bottle and drifts back to sleep. She snores, which makes me nervous. A sable antelope pierces the chest of an attacking lion, wracking its horns to free itself from the flailing claws. I don't know which infant snores are normal, which ones mean Anya can't breathe. I try holding her at different angles, though I know, with the furnace on, the air has been dry and she probably just has mucus in her nose. More animals attack. More die. When I hear Colleen's keys in the lock, we're still in our pajamas.

Colleen looks at us then begins to straighten the framed photos, to fluff the throw pillows. "I told you I'd be here," she says. "Why isn't she dressed?"

"I was having coffee. Anya needed her bottle."

She looks around the living room. "Where are they?"

"Who?"

"The things. The demons."

"I haven't seen them since you called. Maybe the bedroom."

Alarmed, she disappears into the hallway and returns a moment later. "I don't see anything. No twigs, no blood." She surveys the living room again. "Nancy said they tracked blood everywhere. All over her white carpet."

"I haven't seen any blood."

"Why is Anya snoring? Are you holding her right?"

"I'm holding her right, Colleen. I know how to hold her."

"Of course you do," she says, placing the remote controls in a neat row. "What do I know? I only raised four children."

"There's coffee on the stove," I offer. "One of them made it. It's in a saucepan." I start to stand. Colleen holds out a hand to stop me.

"I'll get it, don't worry," she says. "Hold her up higher. Rub her neck a little."

Colleen shuffles into the kitchen. Cabinets open and close, the silverware drawer rattles. The man on the TV is still saying something about animals. I lift Anya to my shoulder and rub her neck. Her snoring stops. I listen for tapping or a shriek from Colleen, but all I hear is the narrator. I close my eyes and count to ten. When Colleen returns with two mugs, I thank her and take a sip. She's strained the grinds and added sugar, which I don't like. I drink anyway, politely, exaggerating an *mmm* in gratitude.

"What's on the table in there?"

"I don't know. Graffiti. A grocery list."

"You can't let them do that. Next thing you know, they'll be doing séances under your bed."

"Séances?"

"Who knows what they do," she says. "Are you watching this?" She turns the channel before I can reply, then sits forward in the recliner with her mug in both hands. These weekend visits—she drives two hours each way. She plans trips to the zoo, the frozen yogurt shop, the park. She pays for everything. I'm still on—paternity leave, they're calling it.

"I said, what are you going to do?" she's saying.

"About what?"

"They'll take your daughter away," she says. "Is that

what you want?"

She finishes her coffee in one long sip.

"I'm her father." And I'm suddenly aware of my daughter's weight in my arms. I hold her closer. Count to ten. "No one is taking her anywhere."

"I'm trying to help you. But they'll bring her to live with me if there are still worries. Should we be worried?"

"Don't worry," I tell her. "I'm going to get dressed."

"You can leave Anya here," Colleen says. "I'm just going to clean up a bit."

"Don't clean anything. Get some coffee. We'll be back in a minute. Everything's fine."

My sheets are shredded. Clothes are in piles on the floor. Carrie's sweaters, skirts, her black party dress—all the things I kept—lie twisted with my suit jackets and jeans. Her picture is face down on the bedside table.

I push the pillows together and lay Anya between them. Her legs kick a little, but she stays asleep. I change into a pair of jeans and a T-shirt, both from the floor. The rest of the clothes I toss on top of the shoes in the closet. Careful not to wake the baby, I check the sheets for signs of blood. As the shreds of sheets unravel, a demon rolls out from under the bed. It yawns and blinks, then crawls up to the photo of Carrie, setting the frame upright and tilting its head as if to apologize. A diagonal crack runs across the glass, and there are scratches on each side of the frame. With both hands, the demon drags the frame across the bed and places it on the pillow beside Anya. Then it pushes some of the shredded strips of linen into a loose nest, curls up next to her feet, yawns, and closes its eyes.

I sit on the bed next to them, watching each body breathe. Anya, belly inflating and sinking. The demon, frayed gills fanning and flattening.

"You've made a mess of everything," I say. "I don't know how to do any of this. I don't know what I'm supposed to do."

The demon and Anya are both asleep. The only face looking at me is Carrie's. The closet doors creak open, and the other two demons skulk into the room. One has my wife's gold bracelet around its neck. Both blink at me, mouths set in guilty frowns.

"What the fuck am I supposed to do?"

Blink. Blink.

"You're not helping."

The one with the bracelet skitters up to me. It lifts the thin gold chain over its head and offers it to me. I slip it into the drawer of the nightstand and notice the pack of cigarettes. In that moment, I want to hold one between my fingers. I want the smell of it, the habit. Something familiar. When I open the box, the cigarettes are missing.

In their place are small seashells, bleached and cracked and sandy. The demon's lips pull back to show a row of dull black teeth. It nods. The scene has the feeling of a ceremony. I smell their bodies and Anya's. Salt and sour milk. The room is quiet, reverent.

"I'm sorry," I say. And I am. When I lift it by its neck, it doesn't squirm or thrash. Its gills flutter against my palm, skin dry and rubbery. It's still smiling. The small body is so light I imagine its bones are hollow like a bird's. The demon purrs, or clears its throat. With my thumb and forefinger, I snap its neck easily. Head falls limply to one side. Gills flag in their rhythm.

I lay it out on the bed next to the sleeping demon and pick up the other one from the closet, breaking its neck the same way as the first. Neither bleeds. The scratched frame I place back on the table where it belongs. Already the first demon's vertebrae are snapping back into place. This is what it knows about death. It hasn't learned it's not supposed to get back up.

When I touch the gills on the sleeping demon's neck, it moves its shoulders as if shrugging off a bad dream. Its skin is cold and dry like the others. I shake it awake. Black eyes fix on the two bodies of its brothers. It shakes its head, disappointed.

"I had to," I tell it. I stand and lift Anya, who's starting to whimper but isn't quite awake. The demon crawls to the others, outlines a symbol on the chest of one of them. As it does this, the necks I've broken are already snapping back into place. "Don't take anything. Please. Don't build a nest or anything in here. We don't need it. We're fine."

Colleen is Windexing the TV. The Bible channel is on now, muted. Colleen circles her paper towel over the faces of a white-suited preacher and a woman in a wheelchair with her arms raised to heaven. Anya wakes as I strap her into her swing—she reaches for Colleen. I hand her a rubber toy whale, and she stuffs the tail in her mouth.

"Did you find them? What happened?"

"Nothing," I say. "I just couldn't find my shoes."

Colleen sprays cleaner on the TV. Anya coughs.

"You don't need to do that."

"It's okay. It'll only take a sec."

"Colleen." My jaw stiffens. I try to count to ten. I only make it to three. "Colleen, right now, drop the fucking Windex."

She freezes mid-wipe, eyes wide. "I'm sorry," she says, looking for someplace to set the bottle. "You know I just want to make sure everything is okay. I don't want you to have to worry about anything."

She means this, I know. She rocked and fed Anya

when I couldn't. She sold the rest of Carrie's things. She reassured the social workers, took care of all the paperwork. Whenever I failed, Colleen was there to make sure things got done, until she was doing everything I should have been.

She looks at me expectantly. She wants to see that I feel something.

"I'm sorry," I say. "I'll get Anya's hat."

She manages a smile. "The pink one. It's the warmest."

Anya's hat is next to her coat and mittens on the changing table. Above the crib, the mobile is spinning. I stop for a moment and watch the fish move in their circle.

Down the hall, I look inside the bedroom. The bodies are gone. The bed is stripped, and fresh sheets are folded in a stack at the end of the bed. The closet door is closed.

And then I see them. They're outside the window. Six black eyes, mouths neutral, showing no teeth. I sit on the bed and watch them for a while until, one by one, they crawl away. When I lock the window, I don't see anything on the side of the building. No pale shapes moving through the parking lot below. The wind smells of car exhaust and autumn leaves.

Colleen is in the kitchen washing the saucepan and the used mugs. She sets all three mugs on a towel to dry, propping the pot against them. Anya is in her high chair with the whale. Spittle hangs between its mouth and hers like a tightrope.

I kiss her forehead. "I love you, baby girl." She gurgles.

On the table, the demon's symbols look like caveman carvings, a museum display. I trace the rough edges with my finger. Maybe, I think, it's a verse from some unholy script or lines from a demon love song. Then I think maybe it's a message. Maybe it's telling me the reason they were here. A good-bye.

"Grow up to be a deep sea diver," I whisper to Anya. "In one of those big Martian-looking suits. Go see whatever there is to see."

I take the coffee jar from the cupboard and scoop some into the filter of the Mr. Coffee.

"Don't worry," says Colleen. "They're not in here. I checked."

"I know."

"We can get a new table. On the way home." She unplugs the drain and dries her hands. "Are you okay?"

"Yeah," I tell her. "We're okay."

I pull the hat over Anya's head. Its flaps cover her ears, and little braids of pink yarn drape onto her shoulders.

She drops the whale and pulls on one of the braids, and the hat twists, its wool flap covering one of her eyes, the other sparkling and blue and looking right at me.

Ghosts of Buenos Aires

*He and the cat were separated as though by
a pane of glass, because man lives in time, in
successiveness, while the magical animal lives
in the present, in the eternity of the instant.*
—Jorge Luis Borges

1

THE PLAZA WAS CROWDED. Too many people drinking café
con leche at the sidewalk cafes, too many pigeons picking
at the crumbs. Tourists shuffled between artisans hawking
small paintings and antique spoons. An old man in a shab-
by suit played tango on the accordion, the tune strange
and stilted without piano or violin, but a small crowd
had gathered around him nonetheless, tossing pesos into
his hat. Emily pushed past them, Luna just ahead of her,
tugging at the leash, the black dog sniffing the cobblestones
and eyeing the pigeons for a chase.

"Luna, no," Emily whispered. "Time to go home."

Instead of heading back down the main drag of Calle Defensa, past the park where the old men played chess under the scraggly arms of the tipa trees, she turned left onto a quieter street, the din of the plaza fading behind her. Later, she would tell herself she was just following the dog, letting her sniff awhile before heading back to the apartment. Rails ran through the bricks of the street, and she tried to imagine a trolley trundling up the narrow thoroughfare, but it seemed too forgotten of an avenue for such a machine.

She was still following the rails when she came to the mansion. It sat behind a high wrought-iron fence, its gate chained and padlocked. The building itself was a crumbling colonial palace, two stories high and sprawling, with a Spanish roof, arched doorways, and tall balconied windows, though any that had not been boarded were broken and dark. The walls were stained gray with soot, and vandals had tagged them with epithets and long scrawls of spray paint. Murals, too, bloomed where there was space: colorful silhouettes of children, a bearded man, a large portrait of a sad woman. In the shadow of the jacaranda trees growing over the fence, the city seemed unnaturally quiet, and Emily stood at the gates, the world hushed, as the old man's distant accordion carried from the plaza, and further off, just a whisper, the heavy traffic of Paseo Colón.

She touched the padlock with her fingertip, tracing its skeleton key opening. Rust flaked away from the iron. "Trick or treat, Lunita," she said. It was almost Halloween, after all, though nothing in Buenos Aires suggested it was the end of October. No pumpkins or dead leaves, no plastic skeletons sneering from doorways as they would be in Milwaukee. The weather was warm, the trees bright and in bloom.

Luna sniffed the gate and whined. In one of the upper windows, something moved. A shape seemed to be there, a darkness within the dark. From the plaza, the old man's accordion faded to a distant hum, the ghost of a melody. She waited for as long as she could, but Luna was pulling, straining in the direction of the apartment. From another window, broken and dark, a white cat slunk onto the balcony and lay in the shadows. Luna barked, but the cat was unfazed.

"Just a cat, baby girl," she told Luna. "Just a cat."

2

At the apartment complex on Uspallata Street, the neighbor girl was leaning against the wall beside the door. She was maybe sixteen, with her long dark hair knotted high on her head with a pink scrunchie. Over her clothes, she wore a white smock, the city's school uniform. Her black pants were Velcroed at the ankles and reminded Emily of something a hip-hop star of the early '90s might have worn. The girl's high-tops were lined with Day-Glo tiger stripes, and in her lip, in imitation of Marilyn Monroe's signature mole, was a white plastic stud. She was listening to American pop music on the speakers of her iPhone, idly chewing her hair. Taking her keys from her hoodie pocket, Emily ventured a smile and an "Hola," but the girl ignored her. She should have been in school—it was a weekday.

"Escuela?" Emily asked, as if it were a question. Luna tried to sniff the girl, and Emily pulled her back.

The girl looked up and said something Emily didn't understand. Then she dropped the phone into the pocket of her smock and walked toward the corner store, where the cartoneros, exhausted from a night of picking recyclables from the city's trash, were finishing their morning beer. Three empty Quilmes bottles lined the sidewalk beside the men. The fourth they passed between them, topping off their plastic cups. The girl disappeared into the little shop, and Emily opened the apartment door.

Amir was making breakfast. Fried rice, again. Three of their four main food groups, he'd say. All they needed was a glass of milk. But the corner store only sold milk in bags, and neither of them had figured out how to pour without spilling. Amir was adding the egg to the rice, a pile of thinly sliced cabbage and carrot waiting on the small cutting board beside the hot plate. Luna bounded toward him, tail wagging, and propped herself against his leg. She leaned her nose toward the sizzling eggs, and Amir calmly pushed her away with a quick tussle of her ears.

"I saw this weird building on our walk today," Emily said. "An abandoned mansion. It's kind of creepy."

He stirred the rice. The eggs weren't scrambled enough. Amir never let the eggs scramble long enough. He was impatient.

"Oh yeah?" he said. "Can we get in? We could throw a Halloween party. How do you say 'Monster Mash' in Spanish?"

"It's padlocked. And anyway, we don't know anybody."

Amir nodded toward the open window. "We could invite the neighbor. I bet she knows all the cool kids." He poured in the vegetables, pushed them around with the wooden spoon. "Woke me up today," he said. "The music on her phone, it carries right up to the window."

His back was still to her. He was shirtless, his skin already a darker shade of brown after only three weeks in the city. In his carry-on, he had brought only books: twenty pounds of them. All the books he couldn't live without, he said. While she spent afternoons searching Craigslist for jobs, he sat with Luna on the terrace, re-reading his favorite books in the hot spring sun. The tattoos on his forearms— lines from poems that wrapped around from wrist to elbow, each rendered in a different typewriter font—blended into his darker skin, difficult to read. As she stared idly at the fading letters, he suddenly turned, smiling. "I almost forgot. I got something."

From the little cabinet by the sink, he pulled a cardboard tray with two paper coffee cups. "It's been three whole weeks since I've had a real cup of coffee. In the cafes, it's all that café con crema stuff. I mean, it's good, but it's like two sips in a hobbit cup. I saw this place when we were out yesterday. Wanted to surprise you."

He was grinning, holding out a cup for her. She wasn't much of a coffee drinker, only drank it when she had exams or papers due. She was surprised that Amir didn't seem to remember that. She took the cup and sipped it as Amir drank his. He immediately spat the coffee on the tile floor.

"Oh Christ. This is worse than gas station shit."

"It's not that bad," Emily said, taking another sip. It reminded her of home, of the store-brand French roast her parents drank every afternoon.

"How can they be so close to Colombia and Brazil," Amir said, "and have such shitty coffee?"

Before she could think of a response, she smelled the smoke. Amir dropped his cup into the sink and grabbed for the burning pan.

"Fuck, fuck, fuck," he muttered, holding it above the

blazing hot plate. "Hand me that spatch?"

She did. Amir scraped at the blackened rice.

"Let's go get pastries somewhere," he said. "And café con crema." Grabbing a shirt, he leaned toward her and kissed her neck. "We can plan our Halloween party."

3

That night, Amir was still in her bed when the ghost appeared. He snored lightly, and she could smell his sweat. She listened to the slow tempo of his heartbeat, her head on his chest rising with each breath. Somewhere in the night, someone was playing the trombone. Long, plaintive notes, and even as she held Amir, she couldn't imagine a lonelier sound. Luna was curled on Amir's bed, deep in sleep, and Emily felt as if she were the only person awake in the world—alone with the sound of a trombone in the night in a strange city. The air had cooled, and she smelled the jacaranda and tipa blossoms from the nearby park and the haze of burnt rice and the sweat and sex soaked deep into the sheets, and then she saw the woman in the darkness.

A white hood obscured her face. On her body hung a tattered blue dress, and webs of dark veins traced their way up her arms and legs. Except for her fingers, each of which seemed to spasm independently, she did not move. Her feet were not feet but gray, sprawling roots like those of the park's big ceiba trees, pushing deep into the checkerboard floor. She was rooted into it as solidly as a centuries-old oak. Luna didn't stir. The trombone stretched out its lonely notes, and the woman stood there, an arm's length from the terrace door, the hood over her face ballooning and contracting as she breathed. Emily was mouthing Amir's name. Then she was screaming it. Her back was against the wall, and the dog was up now and barking, and she was screaming his name, and the ghost was right there and then it wasn't, and she was in a rented room in Argentina, five thousand miles from home, alone, with Amir.

"It was nothing," she said.

Amir handed her a glass of water. "Since when do you believe in ghosts?"

"I don't." Luna nuzzled at her hand, and Emily scratched the dog behind her ears, reassuring her. "I don't know. It's Halloween, right? Spooky season. Must've been a bad dream."

"What'd it look like?" He was sitting next her now, on her bed, his fingers tracing a design on her knee. Her bed, his bed. She had booked the room with two beds without asking him, had known he would be more comfortable if she didn't assume. An unspoken compromise. They'd been sleeping together for months, but not even their other friends knew—or, if they did, politely pretended they didn't. When they walked in, metal cots on separate sides of the room, and he set his bags on one, claiming it without even questioning why there were two, she had felt validated for knowing it was what he wanted, and stung with sadness that she had not been wrong, that he took the separate beds as a given. That he didn't even think to ask why.

"It was a woman," Emily said finally. "She had tree roots for feet."

"Tree roots?" Amir kissed her, and she felt exactly like a ghost—ethereal, rooted to the floor. "You miss Milwaukee. Your mom, your dad, your sister. That's it."

He kissed her again. His fingers moved further up her thigh, and she let them. Luna groaned, stretching off the bed and finding a better place on the cool floor. Amir took the water glass from Emily's hands, leaned her slowly onto the creaking bed, while outside the trombone again began to play.

4

In the morning, Emily didn't look at the spot where the ghost had stood. Just a dream, she told herself. Stress. Strange city, no job. No one in her life but Amir, and all the questions he never answered and she never asked. She changed into jeans and a thin T-shirt, no bra. Amir was in the shower, steam leaking into the room through the doorframe. Even with a towel stuffed against the door, water pooled on the floor outside the bathroom. Through the door, she said, "I'm leaving Luna here."

"Okay," came his response over the sound of water.

Luna lifted her head as Emily grabbed her camera. "Back soon, baby. Keep an eye on Amir." The dog slumped back onto the bed, and Emily stepped out into the marble hallway.

The girl was there, outside her own door, taking long pulls off a bottle of red wine.

"Tu novio es un forro," she said. Her phone was playing music, muffled by the fabric of her smock.

"What?"

"Your boyfriend," said the girl. "Big fucking—" She demonstrated what she meant by grabbing her crotch with her free hand.

"He's not my boyfriend," Emily said. "You speak English?"

The girl shrugged. "Clases de inglés. I watch many movies. American movies."

"Why is he a, uh, Frodo?"

"Forro," the girl corrected, laughing a little. She took another drink from her bottle, then with a nod held it out to Emily. "Asshole. I see him and you."

"He's not an asshole," she said, taking the bottle. It was still morning, but she felt rude not taking it. The girl was making an offering. In this city of three million people, the only friend she had was Amir. She drank from the bottle. The wine was cheap and harsh, metallic. She coughed as she handed it back to the girl. "He's just homesick."

"Nah, puta, oye," said the girl. "'Always reading. Get a job,' mi abuelita says. Al pedo como teta de monja. 'Books is not a job.'"

"It's what he does," Emily said. "He's a writer."

"Reading is not writing, yes?"

Emily was quiet. For a moment, the only sound the tap-tap of a dance song on the girl's phone. "What music are you listening to?"

Light slanted in from the skylights in the hallway, illuminating the young girl in morning glow as she lifted the bottle to her lips. "Nothing. American mierda."

"May I take your picture?" Emily asked. She was already raising the camera to her eye.

The girl laughed. "¿Lesbiana? That why he is not your boyfriend?"

"I'm just taking pictures," Emily said. "Of things in the city. He's sort of my boyfriend. It's complicated."

"Okay, gringa. Whatever you say." The girl posed against the wall, tapping her head back as she gulped from the bottle. She held her fingers out in a peace sign, then extended only her middle finger. She laughed again, a child's laugh despite her attempts to seem older. Emily took several shots, from different angles. She heard Amir's voice in the apartment, and the scuffling of Luna's paws on the floor.

"I have to go," she told the girl. "Thanks for the pictures."

"Copy for me, okay? I want to give them to my boyfriends." The girl smiled. Emily smiled back, and promised she'd make copies.

"What's your name, by the way?" she asked. Then, trying Spanish, "Como te llamas?"

"Agustina," the girl answered. "Agus."

"Agus. I'm Emily."

The girl laughed again. "All American girls are named Emily." She took out her phone, Latin music beginning to play after a few taps on the screen. As soon as Emily was beyond the front steps of the building, the music began to fade, lost to the sounds of the city.

5

The street near the mansion was empty again, except for a single green taxi bumping over the old rails and cobblestones. She looked at the ground until it passed, waiting for the motor's heavy chugging to blend with the distant sounds of traffic and tango. She tried the gate. The chains were rusted, but they held. She thought maybe she could pick it—it was a skeleton-key lock, people in movies always seemed to pick those easily—but she didn't know the first thing about lock picking. She'd never picked a lock in her life. Amir might have known; he might have learned it from one of his books. But Amir wasn't there. He was on the terrace, his shoulders browning, another book in his hands. She dropped the lock, and it clanged loudly against the gate. Several pigeons dislodged from a tree in the mansion yard, settling again on its roof. Emily looked around. Still no one. No one saw her. The fence was too high to climb, nothing but thin wrought-iron bars, topped with spade-shaped spikes and speckled with rust. She took her camera from her pocket and snapped photos through the bars. The boarded windows on the first floor, the broken windows on the second. Political graffiti in black and red spray paint. Pigeons on the cracked roof tiles. She kept clicking until she was sure she had all of it, that she could assemble a collage of the entire building if she wanted to.

"¿Puedo ayudarte, señorita?"

The voice made her jump. A man was standing just behind her. He looked like one of the old men who played chess in the park, short and Italian with a heavy white mustache and thick strands of white hair combed over his liver-spotted scalp. He was smiling. It was a grandfatherly smile.

"Perdón," she said. "¿Inglés? English?"

The old man shook his head. "Cerrado," he told her. "Muchos años."

"Yes," said Emily. "Sí. I understand."

He chuckled and pointed toward the plaza, mumbling something else in his porteño Spanish, heavy on "sh" sounds where the "y" had been in her college language classes. "Sh," as if the citizens of Buenos Aires were telling her to quiet down, keep calm, everything was going to be okay.

"Thanks," she said, too loudly. "Gracias."

He nodded and began to shuffle down the hill, toward the busy thoroughfare of Paseo Colón. She raised her camera, taking several pictures of him until he disappeared beyond the crest of the hill. When she turned back to the mansion, the pigeons were gone, and a white cat was picking its way along a second-story ledge. Emily zoomed the camera in as far as it would go, clicking the shutter button as quickly as it would allow. It was a thick tomcat with dirty, matted fur. Its tail, tipped in black like an ink quill, swayed lazily behind it. She watched it through the pixelated zoom, the cat lying against a broken window pane, stretching its paws, eyeing the pigeons that fluttered from tree branch to tree branch. Behind it, something moved. The cat's back raised suddenly in an arch, and it turned to hiss at its reflection. No: a shadow. Movement, inside. She tried to make out what was behind the dirty glass, but the digital zoom blurred with pixels. The cat made a deep, howling sound and leapt to another ledge, finding its way into a different window. She heard another low howl, and then nothing. Whatever shadow had shifted inside the mansion was gone, the space inside the window occupied by only hollow darkness.

Another cat. It must have been. Cats were everywhere in San Telmo. An abandoned building like that, there must have been dozens. A territorial spat. Cats fought all the time, they were spiteful like that. That's why Emily preferred dogs. Luna always wanted to be loved, no matter what. She wasn't moody. She never sulked or hid away. Her capacity for love was limitless.

6

As the pictures copied from the camera to her laptop, Emily watched Amir through the glass terrace door. He was sitting in a plastic patio chair, Luna lying underneath it. He turned the pages of his book. Occasionally, he reached for a wine glass full of foamy beer. The room only had wine glasses and coffee mugs, and Amir didn't want to drink from plastic cups. She almost laughed; sometimes he could be surprisingly bougie. He topped off the beer from a brown glass bottle, its blue and white label familiar now, even if she couldn't read it from that far away. Around him, houseplants lay dead in their pots; she wasn't sure if she should water them. The woman who owned the apartment hadn't asked her to, and anyway it seemed too late now. They'd gone too long without care. Behind Amir, glass block windows let in marbled light through the concrete walls, and above them, she could see the neighbors' crumbling roofs, half obscured by the reaching branches of jacarandas, their purple blossoms in bloom.

"I didn't know you were back," Amir said, sliding open the terrace door. Luna ran past him into the room, dashing for Emily. She grabbed her dog with both hands, rubbing her fingers through the short black fur while Luna nuzzled her chin.

"I'm back," she said.

"How was the mansion?"

She shrugged, looked at the screen in front of her. "I got pictures."

"Can I see?" he said. He was holding the beer bottle, now empty. His book and glass were still on the table outside.

"I want to edit them first," she said. "I couldn't get close. The gate's locked."

"We need more wine," Amir said. He rinsed the bottle in the small sink and set it on the floor with the other empties. "I'll make pasta later. We can light a candle and pretend we're fancy."

"Okay."

On the screen were rows of thumbnails, the pictures of Agustina at the top. Emily clicked on the first one: the young Argentine girl against the pale yellow wall, wine bottle to her mouth, bright morning light washing out half the frame. Emily scrolled forward, through all the photos of the girl, until she was looking at the mansion. The first was of the curved staircase leading up from the gate. Its tiles were shattered, and shriveled leaves from the previous fall were still stuck in its corners. Next: the heavy arched doors to the first floor. Another chain was padlocked through their iron handles. A sign with CUIDADO printed at the top had been pasted to one of the doors. More photos: the first-floor graffiti, the potbellied palo borracho trees in the yard, the second-floor windows. She saw nothing strange in any of them. In picture after picture, it was just an old building, abandoned and falling apart. Next came the photos of the old man, and she clicked until he disappeared, the last shot simply the empty street with trolley rails cutting through the bricks. Then she was back to Agustina and her bottle of wine.

"That's a nice shot," Amir said behind her. He was holding another liter of beer. "Good lighting."

"Thanks," she said, closing the lid of her laptop.

"If you see her again," he said, "tell her to keep the music down." He stepped out onto the terrace and settled back into the patio chair, Luna trotting out behind him.

7

Emily knew before opening her eyes that the ghost was there. Amir was in his bed, Luna asleep beside him. The window was open. The air smelled of spring flowers and stale beer.

The ghost was rooted again near the terrace door. Thick roots pulsed from her ankles, further into the floor. The dress was muslin, or something just as thin, and there were ruffles on the hems, stained deep with black dirt. Emily could see her breasts beneath the fabric, nipples small and dark, the skin pale. The ghost's arms shook slightly from the movement of her fingers. Behind her, the moon flooded the terrace, and all the plants were still dead, and Emily concentrated on the plants, the realness of them, the details of their decay, the angles of their listing stems. When Amir told her she was dreaming, she would point to the stems and tell him, *I saw this. The plant was dying in this way when the ghost was here.* A bus squealed outside, and she looked toward the window. Only a fraction of a second, but when she looked back, the ghost had moved toward the front door, and next to it, standing naked, his eyes shut tight and mouth wide open, was Amir.

"Amir, Jesus fucking Christ," Emily said. She blinked, and there was only Amir, yawning, and the dog stretching awake on his bed across the room.

"I had to take a piss," he said. He didn't sound sure.

"You were just standing there. With your mouth open."

"I was yawning."

"You were terrifying. You scared the shit out of me."

"Sorry," he said. "Maybe I was sleepwalking."

"You don't sleepwalk," she said. Luna was finding a place on her bed now, moving the blankets with her nose.

"I used to," said Amir, turning on the bathroom light. "When I was a kid."

He didn't bother to shut the door, and she watched him, naked in the light, and listened. She watched him wash his hands and look in the mirror and watch her watching him. He smiled.

"Do you want to?" he said. "I'm awake." He started to walk toward her bed.

She turned over and pulled the blanket over her shoulder. "I'm tired," she said. She could feel him standing there for a moment, heard the light switch click and then his footsteps, the creaking springs of his bed. When she was sure he was asleep, Emily turned off the small lamp and sat in the dark with Luna's head on her feet. She watched the terrace door while the dog and Amir slept. There was nothing to see but the moonlit terrace, the silhouettes of the chair and the table and the sagging leaves of long-dead plants.

8

"Like you said before," Amir said, "it was just a dream."

He was drinking yerba mate from a hollowed-out gourd, just as they'd seen the locals do in the park. He'd given up on the coffee, at least for today.

Emily paced the terrace, looking at each plant, each dead leaf. "I saw this. I was awake and I saw these plants right here. There was something there, Amir. I don't know what it was."

"I know," he said. "But I promise, it's gone now. See? No ghosts." He waved his hand around as if to prove it.

"I saw something else," she said. "At the mansion. I thought it was a cat at first. There's someone in there. Maybe it's connected."

"Maybe. A lot of people in this city are homeless. An abandoned mansion beats sleeping on the sidewalk. Doesn't mean it's haunted."

She didn't know what to say. She hadn't thought of that, of squatters living in the old building. But she wouldn't tell him that; she wouldn't let him be right. She wanted him to believe her. Even if it wasn't true.

"You're right, though. It is connected," he said. "You've been visiting that place every day, creeping yourself out, thinking about ghosts. It's no wonder you're having nightmares."

"Come with me. See it for yourself. There's something wrong with it."

Amir scratched his arm, glancing at the terrace chair. "I can't. I want to finish this book today."

"Why aren't you writing?" she said. "You could at least write something. You're a writer. Now you have the whole day free. No café job taking up your time."

She saw him tense, for a moment. Then he said, "Books are research. I'm looking for inspiration."

There was a whole city of inspiration, she wanted to say. But she knew it wouldn't matter. "If you were just going to read, you could've just stayed in Milwaukee."

"It's cold in Milwaukee. It's probably snowing."

"You know what I mean."

He sucked on the aluminum straw in his gourd, drinking until the tea made a slurping sound.

"I thought this was vacation," he said.

"No, you didn't."

"Well," he said, leaning in to kiss her shoulder, "it's vacation now."

9

Under the heavy morning clouds, the mansion looked nothing like the simple, empty building in her photographs. Cats of different colors crowded the window ledges. So many cats she almost couldn't believe it. Twenty, thirty, maybe more. The white tomcat was on the steps below the front door licking the bent wing of a pigeon, the fur around its nose thick with blood. Luna was barking and jumping at the gates. The chain rattled, but none of the cats so much as yawned. The leash dug into Emily's hand as Luna pulled harder. Shadows from the trees fell heavily on the gates, on the street, on her. A wind blew, carrying a chill from the river, and the tree's reflections scratched across the window panes. She noticed then that every cat was watching her. Not the barking dog or the whispering tree branches—they were looking at her, tails swaying in rhythm, no sound but the trees and the dog, the wind in the leaves practically a roar.

"¿Señorita?" The old man's voice came from behind her again. She recognized its tone. "¿Al perro no le gustan los gatos, no?" He was smiling beneath his mustache.

"No," Emily said, winding the leash around her wrist. "She doesn't like them. No le gustan."

He chuckled. "Sí, sí. Su Castellano está mejorando, señorita. Hasta mañana."

"Wait," she said. He turned, his thick gray eyebrows raised. "Do you know if anyone died in here? A woman? Um…muerte…mujer…vestido azul…en—" she pointed to the mansion, "en la casa?"

The man looked at her. "¿Una mujer muerta?" He shook his head. "Este lugar era para los oficiales. Hace mucho tiempo. A nadie murió acá."

"No one died? Are you sure?"

He smiled sadly and pointed to the windows, and the cats did nothing but lounge on their ledges, indifferent. "Sólo es una casa para los gatos perdidos."

Only a home for lost cats. She managed a smile and thanked him. He nodded and continued his walk, making his way over the hill toward the thoroughfare, having his own morning route to trace. Luna had calmed, distracted by the old man, and Emily turned back toward the plaza before the dog could again notice the cats.

10

A bottle of wine was sitting on the table between the laptops, two clean glasses beside it. A pizza box was open on the counter by the sink, a slice missing. Amir stepped in from the terrace, and the dog bounded around him to greet Emily.

"I got lunch," he said.

"Thanks."

He peeled the foil from the bottleneck and began to twist the corkscrew into place.

"It's too early for wine," she said, suddenly angry. Yawning. He said he had been yawning. And sleepwalking. Months of sleeping together, or in the same room, and he had never walked in his sleep. Sometimes he would grind his teeth, and she would touch his jaw where it hinged to his skull, would rub him there until the grinding stopped and she could sleep again, having saved him from himself. He wasn't sleepwalking. Something strange was happening. This city was making them crazy. Making her crazy.

She needed to relax. A joint would help, though she had no idea where to get one. A job would help too, and, of course, Amir. No more questions, no more wondering. The two of them, out in the world, together.

Amir set the bottle down, corkscrew half stuck. "Okay." He picked up a fat blue book from his bed. "I've been reading Borges," he said. "It seemed like a thing to do, in Buenos Aires. I read this line you might like." He opened to a dog-eared page and read, "*With relief, with humiliation, with terror, he realized that he, too, was but appearance, that another man was dreaming him.*" When he finished, he closed the book and looked up at her with a proud smile.

"Is that supposed to make me feel better?" she said.

His smile faded a little, and he looked uneasy. Good. Let him feel uneasy. "With your dream. I thought you might get a kick out of it."

"My dream," she said. She picked up the wine bottle and finished twisting the corkscrew. She pressed its wings, and the cork pulled free. She poured one glass and drank half in one swallow. "That would be great, if my whole reality were just some other asshole dreaming me. Then they could wake up, and it would be over."

He touched her neck, electric, she felt rooted to the floor. "All right, that was stupid. I'm stupid. I'm sorry. I know you're stressed." He took a slice of pizza out of the box and started to eat. She hated him for it. "We should talk about our Halloween costumes," he said, chewing. "Can't even get a damn plastic mask at the stores here. What should we do? Cut up the bedsheets, go as ghosts?"

Emily listened to the smacking of his lips, the wet grinding of his teeth. She drank the rest of the wine in her glass and took the bottle, turning toward the front door.

"It was a joke," Amir called behind her. Then, sarcastically, "I thought it was too early for wine."

"It's too early for your bullshit," she said, and Luna followed her out the door.

11

Agustina was in the hallway with a boy. It was late afternoon, and she wasn't wearing her school smock, only a thin black tanktop and leggings, her hightops blazing pink on her small feet. The boy was at least a head taller than Amir, with a red polo and white shoes and choppy black hair in a European style.

Over the boy's shoulder, the girl saw Emily and smiled. She closed her eyes and moved her lips to the boy's neck and up, slowly, to his ear, sinking her teeth into the meat of its lobe. From the sudden shrug of his shoulders, Emily could tell it hurt. She pulled a swallow from the bottle and tousled Luna's ears. She wanted to watch the two of them for as long as she could: a moment existed there, between them. She did not want to break it.

Luna barked, and the boy wheeled around. When he saw Emily and the dog, he laughed and blushed. "La puta perra," he said to Agus. "¿Es amistosa?"

"Sí," the girl said. "Este es la famosa yanqui." She laughed, and he laughed with her.

Luna trotted toward them, and the boy crouched to pet her.

"Sorry," Emily said. "Lo siento. I didn't mean to creep on you."

"'Perdón,'" Agus corrected. Then, still laughing, "What is 'creep on you'?"

"Nothing. I just didn't mean to watch." Emily turned toward the door to her room. "Luna," she said, "acá." The dog looked at her but did not leave the boy's petting hands.

"Hey, flaca," Agus called to Emily. She held up one finger. "Un momento." She said the boy's name and whispered to him in quick Spanish, and he stood and kissed her. Pulling away, she smiled. "Chau."

"Chau." With an embarrassed wave to Emily, he headed to the front door and left, Luna curiously sniffing the doorway after he'd gone.

"I'm sorry," Emily said again. She offered the bottle to Agus, and the girl took it. As she was drinking, Emily asked, "Your boyfriend?"

"El chongo," Agus said, swallowing. "El es un chamuyero. Fucking player."

"He seemed nice."

Agus laughed. "Sí, sí. Nice to perras." They both smiled, and Luna loped back to Emily, slumping onto the floor. Handing the wine back, Agus said, "And your chongo? He is reading?"

Emily shrugged. "I don't care."

"You care. You love him."

The bottle was still mostly full. She drank as much as she could in one gulp, then another.

"Tranquila, loca," the girl said. "You will choke."

"Have you ever seen a ghost?" Emily asked.

"A ghost? Sí. Buenos Aires is full of ghosts."

"I mean here. In the building."

"Sí, sí," she answered, nodding. "Muchas fantasmas. Do you see one?"

"I don't know." Emily handed the bottle to the girl. "How old are you? Cuántos años?"

"Your Castellano is very bad," Agus said. "I am old enough." She sipped the wine. "¿Qué—what does your ghost look like?"

"A woman. Blue dress. I couldn't see her face."

"She had no face?"

"She was wearing a hood." Emily rubbed her eyes. "I don't even know if I saw her. It might've just been a nightmare."

Agus shook her head gravely. "Fantasmas are real, gringa. Mi abuelita can talk to them. They are always talking during her telenovelas. She has to turn the sound very loud." Then, conspiratorially, Agus leaned in and said, "I can too." The girl was smiling wide. She had wine on her breath. "The ghosts that want to talk, I can taste them."

"You can what?"

"I can taste them." Agus stuck out her tongue. It was long and purple.

Emily laughed. "Oh yeah? What do they taste like?"

The Argentine girl leaned back. She seemed a little unsteady. "All kinds of things. Vino, cotton, bubblegum." She smiled at Emily. "I will taste your fantasma. If I taste it, I will tell abuelita and she will know what to do."

"Okay," Emily said. She liked how excited Agus was about the ghost. The girl believed her, or seemed to. Even if the girl was joking, it was fun. They were planning something. Conspiring. "Tonight? Dinnertime?"

"Sí," Agus agreed. Opening her door, she said, "Chau, yanqui."

Emily said, "Chau," and sat down to finish the wine.

12

She woke up in her bed to the smell of fresh basil and sweet onion. Amir was making dinner, frying chopped onion and garlic and pulling the leaves from the basil plant in the window to set aside for the sauce. A second pot was boiling water for the noodles, which came wound in little nests in a thick plastic bag. Emily was starving, hadn't eaten anything all day.

"You passed out in the hallway," Amir said, not looking at her. "That girl's grandmother came banging on the door. Luna was curled up next to you, wine was like half gone. The old lady seemed pissed."

Emily sat up. Her head was throbbing. Before she could ask, Amir handed her a glass of water.

"Couldn't find the ibuprofen," he said. "I think it's in your bag."

"Amir," she said.

He turned back to the food. "It's fine. You're seeing ghosts. Anybody seeing ghosts gets a free pass to spaz out at least once. Anyway," he stirred the basil and onion into the pot of bubbling sauce, "we have plans to be fancy. You still game?"

Before she could answer, there was a knock at the front door. Luna barked lazily but didn't bother to leave the bed. Emily and Amir looked at each other as if to ask, *Were you expecting someone?* Or to ask, *Who else do we know in this city?* Amir wiped his hands on a towel and answered the door.

Agus was standing in the hallway blowing pink bubbles with her gum. "Hola, gringos," she said. "Let me see your ghost." She pushed past Amir and looked around the room. "¡Qué pena! Such a small place! ¿Es una caja, sí?" She laughed to herself, went over to hot plate to smell the bubbling sauce. "Qué rico olor."

"Agus," Emily said, "this is Amir. Amir, Agustina."

The girl reached her hand out to shake his. "You love her yet?"

Emily flushed, could feel her chest blazing red. Amir said, "What?"

Agus looked at Emily with almost a wink. "Your ghost. She wants you to love her." The girl sat on Amir's bed next to Luna, scratching the dog's ears. "All woman ghosts—they need the love of a man. Big, strong chupa pija like you. You can save her soul."

"What is she talking about?" Amir said to Emily. His dark eyes were serious, and nervous.

"She came to see the ghost."

"I didn't realize we were the ghost zoo," he said. He glanced at the girl, whose black leggings and T-shirt contoured her young body. "I don't think she should be in here."

"Uh, puedo escuchar, gringo," Agus said.

Amir ignored her. "Em, it was a nightmare. There's no such thing as ghosts."

"How do you know?"

"Right," he said. "How do I know? How do I know there aren't leprechauns or fairies or fucking Santa Claus? They're not real, Em. They're stories."

"You are very sure, gringo," Agus said. "Do you know what is at the bottom of the sea?"

The sauce was bubbling over, and Amir rushed to turn off the flame. He opened the bag of pasta and poured the nests of noodles into the water. "That's not the same. Just because I haven't seen it with my own eyes, doesn't mean I don't know the difference between reality and fantasy. There are no ghosts at the bottom of the ocean. Or here."

"Tal vez," Agus said. She blew a bubble with her gum and popped it with her tongue, then smiled at Emily. "Where is your fantasma?"

"I don't know," Emily said. "She doesn't show up until the middle of the night."

Agus reached for the bottle of wine on the table. "I can wait."

13

For most of the night, the girl talked about her boyfriends. Their number was infinite, it seemed, boys from school and from the university whose names all ended in -o. Amir had settled into one of his silences. He dished pasta onto three plates then took his to the terrace, Luna following at his side. Despite her throbbing head, Emily helped Agus finish the bottle of sweet torrontés, then opened a malbec. She held her glass and let Agus talk. It was easier. If Emily had talked, she would have said something about Amir, and she didn't want to. Not with him there, sulking on the terrace. Not with this young girl, to whom love was still an exciting game.

They almost didn't notice when Amir came back inside. He snapped Luna's leash to her collar and shoved a plastic bag into the pocket of his shorts.

"Where are you going?" Emily asked.

"Out," he said.

"Che, culiao, cuidado. It is dark." Agus was sitting on his bed with her legs bent. She held the wine glass, half empty, on her knee. "There are ghosts all over."

He shook his head, looked as if he would respond,

didn't. Grabbing his key from the small dresser, he left, the door closing hard behind him.

"Ay. Your chongo does not like me."

"It's just the ghost thing." Emily poured herself more wine, then offered the bottle to the girl. "Amir doesn't believe in anything. He's too practical."

"Moving to Buenos Aires with a woman he does not love is practical?" Agus asked. "Reading books all day, no job, is practical?" She laughed. Emily laughed too, though the first question had stung—it was too close to the question she'd been asking herself, the question she was afraid to ask Amir. She did not want to know the answer. If he said it, it would be real. And then it would be over.

"You know what I mean. He doesn't even like fortune cookies. He thinks the fortunes are a waste of time." Setting her glass on the table, she said, "Your grandmother is going to hate me. Getting her granddaughter drunk on a school night. Is that illegal?"

"No le diré nada," Agus said as she mimed locking her lips and throwing away the key. "She is watching her shows. She does not miss me. She will say at least I am not with a boy. Abuelita hates boys." The girl looked into her glass as she drank. "I like this wine."

"Amir bought it."

"It's making me cansada."

"You can sleep. I'll wake you up if I see anything."

Then Emily said, "Can you taste it?"

"El vino? Sí."

"The ghost," Emily said. "What does my ghost taste like?"

The girl stuck out a wine-stained tongue. She moved it around, left to right, up and down. Her lips shined wet, and there was a small purple stain on her bottom lip, a kiss from the Malbec. "No puedo saborear nada, Emmy."

"I thought you could. I thought you tasted them."

"Sí, sí. Los fantasmas that want to talk."

"And the ghosts that don't?"

"They taste like wine."

Agus set her glass on the dresser and let herself fall sideways onto the bed, still wearing her high-tops. She pulled Amir's blanket up over herself. Emily emptied the rest of the wine into her own glass.

"Wake me up, mina," the girl said. "If la fantasma comes."

She drifted into sleep, and Emily watched her, the girl suddenly looking so young and vulnerable, her hard exterior sloughed like a crab shell. Emily felt guilty then, having given her so much wine. She took the girl's glass to the sink and washed it, unsteadily, as if the washing would take it back, would wash the wine out of the girl. She set the glass on the towel to dry. Amir wasn't back, and it was dark. They both had been told not to be in the park after dark, that it was a different place when the sun set. Especially for gringos. She held her glass with both hands and watched the girl sleeping in Amir's bed, small chest rising and falling, thinking she had never slept so peacefully in her life, or at least not in Buenos Aires, which now seemed so much like her life that it was difficult to remember any other. Somehow, her glass was empty again. And the space beside Agus, in this bed that was Amir's, was close and warm, and she was in it then, beside the girl, above the blanket because she would not stay long, only long enough to rest her eyes.

14

In the dream, she was standing on a beach. The wind was blowing. She knew a city was behind her, but she could not turn around to see it. Everything depended on her not looking at the city, and if she saw even one building, one traffic light or park bench, the world would collapse. Amir stood in the waves with his arms up. He was reading his tattoos in the proper sequence. The wind was so loud. It blew sand into her throat as she tried to tell it to stop. She could only hear wind and waves, and tasted earth when she called his name. If he said the last line before the wind died, she would never know, and again she asked the wind, and again her throat was sand and she did not have a voice in that world, and the silver waves roared. Amir let his arms drop, his litany complete, and she woke in the room next to the teenage girl, in the dark, with sand on her tongue.

In the dim moonlight, she could see that the dishes were all washed and stacked on a towel. The empty wine bottles were on the floor beside the trash. Amir was in the other bed with Luna at his feet, and the ghost was sitting next to him, her roots coiling around the leg of the bed frame.

Instead of screaming, Emily closed her eyes and stuck out her tongue. She felt silly; she knew it must have been a joke, a prank on the foolish yanqui. She tasted her own breath and the old-sock feeling the wine had left in her mouth. When she opened her eyes, the ghost was still there.

"Don't touch him," Emily whispered. "Please."

The white hood turned, inflating, deflating, inflating. No eye holes had been cut, but Emily could feel it watching. "What's your name? Who are you?"

The ghost's fingers twitched.

"Did you live in the mansion?" Emily asked. "Did you live here?"

Below the ghost's bruised ankles, the thick roots grew, and her thin arms looked, from this angle, so much like the limbs of trees. Perhaps it was some sort of Hellenic metamorphosis—like Daphne or Syrinx. Perhaps in a thousand years she would only be the ghost of a tree. Emily sat up, and the woman looked less plantlike, more human again—a pale, hooded woman in a blue dress with ceiba roots for feet.

Emily touched Agustina's small shoulder.

"Agus," she said. "She's here. Fantasma." She said it as if it were a name. An invocation. But when she looked back, the ghost was gone. She hadn't even realized she'd looked away. The ghost was gone, and in her bed were Luna and Amir, and in his bed were herself and the teenage girl from across the hall in this shitty apartment building in Buenos Aires. She started to laugh. She kept laughing, because as long as she laughed she wouldn't cry.

"Emmy? What are you, crazy?" Agus was leaning up in the bed, shedding the blanket.

Still laughing, Emily said, "Do you taste anything?"

The girl rubbed her eyes. "Sí, mierda. I need to brush my teeth." She crawled around Emily, out of the bed. "Abuelita is going to kill me."

"I'll tell her we were studying English and you fell asleep."

"How will you tell her? She does not speak English."

"I'll write a note."

Luna was awake then, and stretched off the other bed, walking lazily across the room. She found the space Agus had left warm and curled up in the ruffled blankets. The girl closed the door behind her, and Emily folded herself around the dog and into sleep.

15

The next morning, Amir didn't make breakfast. She found him on the terrace with Luna, the French press empty on the table beside his cracked mug. Luna rubbed against her leg, but Emily did not crouch to pet her: she wanted to be standing. He pretended to read as she stood over him.

"What the fuck was that," he said finally.

"What was what?" she said.

He closed the book, his thumb marking his place. "That girl? Feeding her drinks? Both of you passed out in my bed when I get back from walking your dog?" He shook his head, an ugly look on his face. "It's irresponsible. Maybe dangerous. We could go to fucking jail for giving alcohol to minors."

"Everyone drinks wine here."

"I don't want her here," he said. "I don't want people around here getting ideas. We already stand out."

"What ideas?"

"It's weird," he said. "You've been weird. Since we got here. Seeing ghosts. Getting drunk with kids."

She stood looking at the plastic corner of the chair just beyond his shoulder. She would not look at him. And she would not say anything. She would stand there in silence with her eyes on the chair back forever if she had to. Or until he said something else.

"I've been thinking," he said, "about going home."

She reached down and touched the dog. "Then go."

"I mean both of us. We're not getting jobs. School's out, the city's on vacation. Nobody needs an English tutor. Let's go back home. At least we can say we tried."

Luna panted in the heat, her black lips curled into a smile. Maybe he was right. Things had been worse since they left Milwaukee. Or maybe she was just finally noticing, seeing all of the cracks, the two of them, like Amir's mug, ready at any moment to shatter.

"Yeah," she said. "Yeah, maybe."

When he stood up and touched her arm, he looked like a stranger, someone she'd known in some other life. His beard was growing out, his tattoos fading, his cheeks and ribs more defined after nearly a month of fried rice and cheap wine.

"We could get a place in Bay View. I could go back to work at the coffee shop, you could freelance, maybe even teach." He was holding her now, and she could feel his heart beating fast. He smelled like his sweat and like coffee, and she loved it, wanted to breathe him in and feel him inside her body, inside her chest and lungs. "Let's go home, Em."

She breathed, his smells filling her, thinking about nothing except the movement of her chest and his. If she said anything, it could break the spell. Then, gently, she stepped out of his arms and reached for the French press.

"I need coffee."

Inside, she emptied the grinds into the trash. Water boiled quickly in the small tin teapot. She watched the steam rise out of it and thought, for a moment, that she must be going crazy. He had said what she had silently begged him to say. Not just these few weeks, but for months, since their first night together, since before that, when they were friends, trading poems between classes and watching the maple seeds fall in circles to the sidewalks and sneaking onto the beach of the lake at night to listen to the waves. All of that, before, it felt so far away now, another life. It had only been three weeks, a little more. She could go back. He was right, there were jobs. Family, friends. Everyone spoke English. She knew she should want to buy a plane ticket that afternoon, fly back with Amir, and be happy. And she knew, too, that she couldn't. She would tell Amir to go. She would be okay if he left, she told herself; in fact, she would be better. Her hand in an oven mitt, she poured the boiling water over fresh grinds in the press and knew she wouldn't be. Without him, she would dissolve in this city. She would blow away into the river.

16

After Luna's walk, Emily waited on the front stoop of the apartment building. She drank beer from a plastic cup like the cartoneros, and Luna lay curled at her feet, pricking her ears up now and then when she heard a distant bark or the whining brakes of a bus on Calle Bolívar. She wasn't ready to see Amir, and she needed to ask Agus about the night before. Maybe the girl remembered something, had seen the ghost in her half-sleep. Maybe she knew the history of the mansion, or would brave the fence with her to see what was inside.

The girl's grandmother stood over her, breathing, as if considering which direction to turn.

"Hola," Emily offered. Sitting, she wasn't much shorter than the old woman. The grandmother had the stout body of an Italian woman who'd borne too many children. She wore black slacks and a funereal sweater, even in the heat. Around her neck hung a gold cornicello amulet. She looked down at Emily the way she might've looked at bread mold or a hair in her empanada.

"Usted es la abuela de Agustina, no?" Emily tried. She knew already, had seen them together carrying groceries, the old woman then walking alone toward the bus stop on Sunday mornings.

The woman muttered in Italian-accented Spanish and shook her head, the white hair so short and tightly curled it did not move. She pulled the building's front door heavily and negotiated herself inside, letting the iron door slam behind her. Luna jumped and growled a little, but Emily calmed her with a hand on her ears and a quiet whisper of "Sí, Lunita, sí, sí, Lunita."

A door whined, and Amir was slumping next to her.

"Let's go," he said, taking her hand.

"Where?" she asked, certain he meant Milwaukee, home.

"The haunted house. Show me."

17

The mansion loomed behind the old gates. Luna pulled on her leash at the sight of the cats, and above them, through the canopy of palo borrachos and jacarandas, moved flat gray clouds. Emily kept her eye fixed on the viewfinder of her camera, zoomed in as far as she could go. It was not yet dusk, but the sun was hidden, muting the light. Plenty of shadows, but none of them moved. Over the sounds of the cats and Luna and the distant traffic, she thought she heard the trombone.

"Zombies," said Amir. "We could be zombies. Rip some old clothes, powder our faces. It would be the easiest thing."

"Do you hear that?" she said.

"The trumpet?"

"Trombone."

"Probably the plaza." Amir gestured toward the street then leaned on the gates. "One of the tourist bars by the park has a couple of skeletons in the window. They're doing a Halloween thing tomorrow. We should go."

Emily searched for the white cat. It sat half in a shadow on the second floor, one paw hanging off the ledge. It watched, as it always did. From that distance, she couldn't be sure the stain on its face was blood.

"What do you think?" Amir was looking at her. "Zombie boy, zombie girl?"

"I don't have any old clothes," she said. "I only packed stuff that I wanted."

"I packed some stupid shit. Winter stuff. I'm not going to need it."

"You're going?"

He smiled, embarrassed. "I thought we were? I thought we talked about it. We could stay a few more weeks, enjoy the sunshine, then hop a plane back before the money runs out. We'd be back before Christmas."

"We could stay here," she said. "We could try."

Amir rattled the padlock on the gate. "Maybe your ghost lived here. You should ask her. It looks like a ghost house."

"I thought it was just a dream."

"It is," he said, "but dreams can be powerful. They can reach out—" He touched her shoulder, fingertips brushing her neck. "And grab you." Her breath caught in her throat, and something sparked just below her belly button. Sparked again. He was touching her, not in the middle of the night, in the secret of their room, but on the street, in broad daylight. His whisper was warm on the flesh of her ear. "Let's head back."

Over his shoulder, she looked for the white cat again, to say goodbye. But it wasn't on the ledge. None of them were. The yard around the mansion was empty. The cats—every one of them—had disappeared.

18

Emily did what she wanted. Their clothes were on the floor of the small apartment, and the window was open, but she didn't care. Each time he tried to move her, on the creaking bed, she would hold his wrists and slide him further into her, watching him surrender. After, they lay naked on the sticky sheets, passing a warm liter of beer between them. She watched his arms move, lean muscle under brown skin, as he handed her the bottle.

"I've been looking at places," he said. "For when we get back. There's one in the Third Ward—hardwood floors, these old crystal doorknobs, right above a brewpub. Dogs allowed." He smiled at her, and Luna looked up from where she was moping on the floor. "No ghosts."

The beer frothed in her mouth, mixing on her tongue with the taste of his sweat. She'd have to wash the sheets now. Or not. He could wash them. She could take his sheets, his bed. He could sleep in the mess.

"Room for two beds?" she said.

His eyes looked somewhere else—the window, the sink, the terrace. "One bed," he said. "One big-ass bed. Big enough for Luna too."

The beer bottle was heavy in her hand, and she wished it were cold. Outside, bright afternoon light fell across the terrace, all the plants lying dead in their own peculiar angles, the single plastic chair in the middle of it, a book butterflied on its seat.

"Why is it so hard for you? To be here, with me."

She felt him turn to look at her, his fingertips on her stomach, on her thigh. "Because the beds are too small."

"I mean it. Why is it hard?"

"It isn't. It's the easiest thing in the world."

"You're not here. Not really."

He breathed. One breath, two. "I don't know, Em. I'm trying."

She sat up and tipped the bottle. The warm bubbles foamed in her mouth, out of it, dribbling down her chin, onto her chest, her body. Grabbing the bottle, he laughed, his thumb wiping away the foam on her lips.

"Slow down. It's only, like, two."

"It's vacation, isn't it?" She smiled so he wouldn't take offense.

"Yeah," he said. "Our winter in Buenos Aires."

❦

They were still in bed, had left only to pick up a small pizza and another liter of beer, when someone knocked on the apartment door. Emily pulled one of Amir's T-shirts over her head while he struggled to find his shorts. Luna barked half-heartedly from the floor.

"Don't offer her beer," Amir said.

She smiled. "It's rude not to share."

Finally, Agustina had come back. Emily needed to ask her about the ghost, about the mansion. She wanted, too, to tell the girl about Amir, about going home.

"Agus, I thought—" she began opening the door. Instead of Agus, the old woman thudded into the room. Amir scrambled to cover himself. She wondered what he would think. Would he laugh it off, or would he sink into silent resentment, thinking this was her fault, payback for getting the woman's granddaughter drunk? The old woman clutched a smoking smudge of sage in one hand. In the other, a pearl rosary. Scented smoke filled the room as the grandmother waved the sage in each corner. She mumbled in Italian, ignoring Emily and Amir. Luna sniffed the old woman and the smoke, suddenly quiet.

"Agustina told you?" Emily said. "De… la fantasma?"

The old woman frowned and kept brandishing the sage. She kept her distance from the Americans. It was as if they weren't even there.

"La fantasma?" Emily said again. "The ghost? Do you

feel it? What are you doing?"

"She doesn't know what you're saying," Amir said.

"You don't know that."

"Either way," he said, "she isn't listening."

The old woman cast a glance from the corner of her eye but kept to her work. She muttered the whole time. Emily listened for any words she recognized. The sage smelled wonderful and otherworldly and reminded her how hungry she was.

"She comes at night," Emily told the woman. "She seems sad. I can't see her face, but I feel that she is. She has to be."

The old woman turned to face her. "No más," she said. She stormed toward the door, rosary clutched in her small fist. "¿Sí? No más. No más. No más." Sage smoking in front of her like a torch, she barreled into the hallway and disappeared behind her own front door.

"We're cleansed," Amir said. "Ghosts no más." He wrapped his arms around her, pulling at the hem of his shirt on her body. "Let's get another beer."

19

Naked she waited. For the ghost, for Agus. She listened for the girl's loud laugh, the tiny echo of music, for the door of her grandmother's apartment to open and close. She listened for the trombone and for cats mewling in the darkness. Amir snored beside her. A third bottle of Quilmes lay empty on the floor, and she felt drunk and confident and good and bad and sorry that she let the old woman send the ghost away. She thought about what Amir had said, the apartment with the doorknobs. One bed. She couldn't tell if he was serious, or if he was just talking that way because they were naked and drunk and he sometimes talked like he loved her, when they were like that, alone together. She wondered, too, what could have changed, and if he was just saying what she wanted to hear so that she would go back with him, back to Milwaukee and how things had been there, complicated and uncomplicated at the same time. Sometime in the night, she got up and opened a bottle of wine, drank only a sip before pouring it down the sink.

"Luna," she said. The dog was awake, looking up with forlorn eyes. Dogs know. "What should we do," she asked. "Do you want to go home?"

The dog's tail twitched.

"I'm sorry. I'm sorry I brought us here."

The dog breathing. One breath, two.

Emily listened again for the sounds she wanted to hear, for anything. Any sound to stop her from talking, from saying secret things out loud. The street below was so dark she couldn't see it. A streetlamp out, maybe fog.

"I can't just keep doing this. What fucking is it even. What am I doing."

And there, in the distance, was the trombone. A slow, jazzy solo drifting in the darkness like oil. She listened to the melody, the long notes of it, familiar now—always, she realized, the same. She closed her eyes, and the solo hit the same note, the same note, longer, louder, louder still until it was right there in the room, an impossible note, a note that was at the same time within her and filling every space of the apartment, a note so loud and deep it would make her chest explode.

When she opened her eyes, Amir was still asleep, grinding his teeth. Luna's back legs kicked, dreaming of movement. In the morning, it would be Halloween, was in fact Halloween already, midnight already past. It seemed ridiculous, playing at ghosts when she'd just sent one away. Playing at terror when she'd been so afraid. Outside, there was no music. Not even the faint traffic noise of the thoroughfare a few blocks away. As she pulled on her clothes in the dark, she heard the creaking wheels of a cartonero's cart, glass clinking, the soft grunting sounds of someone hard at work. She clicked the leash onto Luna's collar, and touched her ears to wake her.

"It's Halloween, baby girl," she whispered. "We have somewhere to be."

20

The mansion was bright with moonlight, the palo borrachos and jacarandas glowing nearly white. The moon itself was fat and wide among the clouds. On the street, streetlamps cast long shadows on the cobblestones. A lone cartonero, her cart pulled by a thin mule, picked through a stack of trash. Seeing Emily, she stopped her work and whispered to the mule, leading it back toward the plaza.

Emily gripped Luna's leash, shaking the gates with her free hand to test their lock.

"Lunita," she said aloud, "how are we going to get in?"

The black dog sniffed at a stain on a fat brick.

"That might do it."

She hefted the brick, looking around to make sure the quiet street was still empty. The chains were rusted, but they were still metal, and the brick thudding against them made a clang that cracked the night and made her arms shudder. She looked for any movement on the street, or behind the gate. But for the barking dog, she was alone. On the third hit, the chain gave, and the heavy lock dropped to the pavement. The doors creaked open, rust falling from their hinges. Emily stood in the open gate, the space between in and out. Luna pulled, away from the mansion and the trees.

"Cállate," Emily said. "It's okay, baby girl."

She stepped inside, feeling as if she were walking through a cemetery or someplace equally silent, and hallowed. The front door and windows were boarded, save for one, in which she could see a dim light—moonlight, maybe, illuminating a courtyard inside. Luna whined but followed, leash slack. Emily tried to loosen her own grip on the leash, knew she should take the dog's reticence as a warning. She took comfort, at least, in Luna being there; the boxer in her made her muscular and gave her head a square shape some mistook for a pit bull.

The window opened into a small room with crumbling plaster and splintered marble tile and a rusted bedframe without a mattress. Cobwebs draped low, and Emily had to duck to make her way toward the open door. Small, desiccated forms huddled in the corners, some of them too large to be mice.

"It's okay, Luna, it's okay," she whispered, more to herself than the nervous dog.

Beyond the door lay a kind of ballroom with a grand staircase ascending on the far side. Above the stairs, a section of the roof had caved in, plaster and wood and concrete wrecked in chunks and angles, and the moon visible through the hollow. Remains of furniture—a sagging wingbacked chair, a toppled table—sat in unnatural places, as if they'd grown there rather than been placed by human hands. Emily blinked, eyes still adjusting to the low light.

Luna huddled at her knees. Wallpaper peeled like skin, and here and there were the remnants of small fires and vagrants' bedding, and crisscrossing maps of paw prints in the dust.

She knew then that she shouldn't have come. That she should be in bed with Amir, in his arms. She knew, too, that she'd had no choice. And that being with Amir, feeling him close, was a kind of dream, one that she was slowly blinking away. She sneezed, and then she saw it: a small patch of blue-white in the darkness. As her eyes adjusted, she could see that it was the hood, the ghost sitting on the edge of a moldering sofa in the middle of the collapse and chaos of the mansion. Around her, wreckage and beams piled on the floor.

Is this real? Emily didn't want to say it out loud—to risk stirring the ghost, or someone else spending the night in the mansion's rooms. But finally, walking slowly across the room, she said, "Are you real?"

The ghost didn't answer.

As she neared, she saw the familiar body. White hood, blue dress, dark veins lacing the exposed gray skin. The hood ballooned and deflated in regular rhythm. Below her knees, her legs were no longer recognizable as legs. Pale wood stretched into the floorboards, roots splayed and seeking. Her fingers had become roots, too, small runners creeping down from her knuckles.

The dog sniffed at the roots in the floor, head low.

"It's okay, Luna."

The hood turned, the impression of a face beneath the fabric aiming toward her. "Luna," said the ghost from beneath the hood. Her voice was Agustina's. "You name your dog after the moon."

"You're not her," Emily said. "You're not Agus."

"Cálmese, yanqui," the ghost said, almost laughing. "You think too much. You are on vacation, no? Relax."

"You're not. Just tell me that. Tell me you're not."

The ghost twitched her fingers, roots brushing the ragged hem of her dress. "'Soy el otro tigre, el que no está en el verso.' Don't worry. I am nothing. I have been nothing for a long time."

Emily looked at every angle of the body of the ghost, reassuring herself that the slim shoulders, the bony knees, were nothing like those of her young and healthy neighbor. She felt a thousand questions rattle her teeth, and the urge to ask none of them, to stand there, with the ghost, for as long as it would exist. Luna leapt onto the space beside the ghost and curled up, dust on her nose, and the ghost ventured one slow pet with her long, crooked root-fingers.

"If you're not Agus, then who are you? Why have you been showing up in my apartment? What can I do to help you?"

The ghost shrugged. Her skin looked wet with sweat, though the air was cold enough for a sweatshirt, early spring. "You ask boring questions."

"Take your hood off."

The hood shook. "Why don't you sleep, gringa? Why do you waste your time with ghosts?"

Emily looked around the old, broken room. "Where are the cats? There are usually so many cats here."

"Cats go where they go."

"What happened to your legs?"

"What happens to everyone, in time. When one is unsure how to move them."

Beside the ghost, Luna lifted her head and began to growl. Picking its way down the fallen beams of the ceiling was the white cat, a fresh kill—a bird, perhaps—in its teeth.

"Luna, no," Emily said, and the dog obeyed, for the moment. She half expected the ghost to disappear, to be gone after every blink, but the hood kept ballooning with breath, and the small shoulders shuddered as if chilled. "Just tell me something. Anything."

Luna stood, hackles raised. Behind the white cat, from all over the house—the roof, the second floor, even the shadows of the ballroom—the other cats emerged. All of them, stepping into the moonlight, eyes on Emily and her ghost.

The ghost coughed, and a spatter of red darkened the hood.

"Are you okay?" It came out of her mouth even as she knew how ridiculous it was to ask.

"Muerta," the ghost laughed. "Sure, okay." Then, after a strained breath, "Roots are strong. They can break stone, when they need to."

The dog jumped from the sofa, barking. The cats, in their mass, did not move, did not react at all. Their eyes followed Emily. She held tightly to the leash, felt it strain against her hands. She waited for the ghost to leave, to dissolve into the air like dandelion seeds, but the ghost stayed. The ghost sat on the sofa, straining to breathe, fingertips curling toward the floor and taking root between the boards. The pale wood no longer stopped at her knees; it had climbed further up her legs, disappearing under her dress, and Emily could guess what would happen next, given time.

"I'm sorry," she said. "I wish I could do something."

"Que nada," said the ghost, turning her hooded face toward the cats. "It is a natural thing."

Emily hesitated, but Luna's pull was strong. She wasn't sure how much longer she could hold on, or what the dog would do if it were free. With both hands, she dragged Luna away toward the small room and the window with the missing board. Behind her, she sensed the movement of a thousand paws, but she did not look back.

21

Medialunas and café con crema. Sunlight so thick and white she could've put it in her coffee. The morning passed slowly, outside time, the two of them in bed after the brief walk to the cafe, Amir talking about his barista job, the one he would return to, and the best way to make a cappuccino, how the milk had to be cold and just so.

"I'm shit at making cappuccinos," he said. "I can't really do it. But that's the industry secret. Extremely confidential."

She let him talk. As long as he was talking, she didn't have to think or say anything. As long as he was talking, they were there, together, and he wasn't on the terrace with his books and she wasn't staring through the gates of a haunted house. Luna groaned now and then, an alert that she was ready for a walk, overdue, but she would have to wait.

"Happy Halloween, by the way." He bit her shoulder, gently. "What are we going to do? Trick-or-treat in the plaza?"

You were right, she wanted to say. *We could both be ghosts.* She was thinking of the mansion and the hooded woman turning quietly into wood, the thousand cats, the voice so much like the girl she'd met in the space between their apartments. It seemed like a dream, the edges of the memory already beginning to unravel. Only the dust on her shoes, the cobwebs on Luna's fur convinced her it had been real. She'd broken into the empty mansion, and the ghost had been there, as real as the plants lying dead in their pots.

"I love you," she said. "You need to know that."

"What?"

"I love you."

"I know," he said.

"Just tell me," she said. "Tell me so I don't feel crazy."

"What do you want me to say? Of course I love you."

"Why are you even here? Why did you fly all the way here, to Buenos fucking Aires, just to fuck me and sleep in your own bed and act like everything is the way it's supposed to be?"

"I don't know," he said. "You were leaving. I didn't know what else to do."

She waited for him to say something else.

"We can go back," he said. "Get a place together, go to the lake on weekends."

"On your terms. We can be together if it's the way you want to be."

"That's not fair. We're struggling here."

"You're struggling. I'm fine."

"We still don't have jobs. You're seeing ghosts. Waking up terrified. Getting the teenage neighbor drunk. That isn't fine."

She said, "It's not enough. Your way, it's not enough. It's a glass cage."

"Jesus, Em. Don't be so fucking dramatic."

"I'm not going," she said finally. "I want you to go. You'll be happier there. But I'm not leaving, not yet."

Amir blinked, stiffened, already the walls building back up. "I thought it was what you wanted. Us, together."

Part of her wanted to tell him it was, and she'd go, and they could get that stupid apartment in Milwaukee with the doorknobs, whatever he wanted. She wanted nothing else to matter, but it all mattered, the force of everything filling the space between them like a tidal wave. "Go home, Amir."

He sat on her bed, and Luna lifted her head, nudging it onto his lap. He didn't touch her, did not seem to even notice. He looked at his hands as if reading a book that was no longer there. "What will I do?"

She knew he meant Milwaukee, but she said, "We'll dress up in our own clothes, go to the bar with the jack-o-lanterns in the window, and drink as much wine as we can. After that, you'll buy a plane ticket."

"Costumes straight out of Wearing Your Own Clothes magazine," he said. "I can go as the guy who just got kicked out of Buenos Aires."

"You can be a zombie," she said.

"That's not much better."

But he was smiling now, and so was she, the mood softening in the warm light. She took another medialuna from the bag and savored the flaky pastry, the glaze sticky on her fingers. He would go. She would stay. It was as if they had always known, a truth that had always been true but unnamable until she named it. The taxonomy of their lives. They would drink wine in bad costumes and make love and sleep together in one of the small beds because there were no more questions, no what-ifs, just the two of them, waking from a dream.

22

The stoop outside the apartment building was quiet. Only a few blocks away, costumed tourists were dancing in the plaza, wine spilling from plastic cups onto the cobblestones. But there, on the little tree-lined street, Emily could hear nothing but the sounds of distant traffic and barking dogs, the occasional passing bus. She listened for the trombone, gave up after a long silence with none of the familiar notes. Amir lay asleep—passed out—in one of the beds inside, his makeup and zombie blood smearing the sheets. After one cup of wine, he'd started taking shots of fernet with an

Australian Dracula, and she'd had to nearly drag him back home. The apartment still stank of vomit. She was thankful for the fresh air.

"Hey, flaca," she heard, and almost expected to see the ghost. Agustina walked clumsily up the sidewalk in heeled boots. As she got closer, Emily could see her makeup in the light—an immaculate sugar skull design, with her hair teased wild. Agus said, "What are you supposed to be?"

Emily looked down at herself, though she knew exactly what she was wearing: a black sweater, black jeans, a cheap pet collar. Black costume makeup on her nose and streaked along her cheeks. "Luna."

"¿La perra? You look like a cat."

"Luna has whiskers."

"Si. Dots. Polka dots. That is how you make dog whiskers." The girl sat beside her on the stoop, her backpack slumped between her feet. She smelled of wine and cigarettes and, underneath, a floral perfume. "Abuelita told me, your ghost—gone. Como si fuera algún tipo de rosa."

"Yeah. I think so." She didn't want to tell Agus about the mansion. She didn't want to have to explain that the ghost spoke in the girl's voice, that she'd explained nothing, that the room tasted only like dust.

"Tu chongo, he is not doing the Halloween too? ¿Truco o trato?"

"He's going home."

The girl frowned. "You are leaving soon?"

"Not me," Emily said. "Just him."

Agus nodded. "Entiendo." Then, with a smile, "Very practical," and Emily smiled too. The girl turned and started to rifle through her bag, pulling out a corked wine bottle. "You want some? It's good. I took it from this party."

"No, thanks."

The girl shrugged, then took a swig, coughing as she swallowed. "Qué pena. I think I took the wrong bottle."

A bus passed at the end of the block, and the girl drank more wine, and Emily thought of the first time she had seen the ghost, how her thin fingers had moved in the dark.

"It's late," Emily said, standing up. "Amir's going to be hungover tomorrow."

"To hangovers," said Agus, raising the bottle, a salute. She grinned her skeleton grin, lips painted like teeth.

❧

Amir looked dead, though she knew it was just the make-up. Moonlight flooded in through the terrace windows, making the white paint on his face almost glow. His jaw twitched, a movement that, in the half-light, the pale skin, reminded her of the ghost woman's hands. Emily almost touched him, and didn't. Instead, she found an empty trash bag in a box beneath the sink.

The door to the terrace creaked, and Luna's ears pricked up, though the dog did not stir from the foot of his bed. Outside, Emily breathed the night air—crisp and full of spring blossoms and cooking smoke from a nearby parilla grill and distant, hazy notes of traffic smog. She could hear buses and faraway club music and the tin beats emanating from Agus's phone not far beyond the wall. The first plant she chose was the smallest, some kind of succulent. The kind of plant that was supposed to be tough enough to survive without regular water. Its tips were shriveled, looking black in the dimness. She dropped it into the trash bag and picked up another, dumping the plant and its soil, setting the pot back on the concrete in case the woman who owned them wanted to replant. With some work, new plants could thrive. The terrace got plenty of light during the day.

When the last plant had been dumped, she hauled the bag out to the curb, passing the skeleton Agus and her stolen bottle. The girl was leaning over, gloved hand stroking a cat without a collar.

"It is you," Agus said, nodding toward the cat. It was a thin calico, heavy splotches of red and black enveloping a belly of white. "What are you throwing away?"

"Some old plants." Emily sat beside the girl, reached

a hand out for the cat to sniff. The cat nudged her fingers plaintively, whiskers tickling just a little. "Where did the cat come from?"

Agus shrugged. "Las sombras. She just came. She likes you."

Emily ruffled its ears, felt the topography of its bones as she smoothed a hand over its back. She wondered if it was one of the legion she had encountered at the mansion, one of the endless cats behind the white tom, and she knew she would never know, and that it didn't matter. The cat stretched itself beyond her touch and sniffed the bag of dead plants. Then it ambled down the street toward the park, existing perfectly in the moment, an impossible thing.

Acknowledgments

Thank you to the following people for their help in making the stories in this collection possible: Michael W. Cox at the University of Pittsburgh at Johnstown, Sam Ligon and Gregory Spatz at the Eastern Washington University MFA program, Jessica Lakritz, Greg Leunig, Jason Sommer, TJ Fuller, Rachel Engelman, Dave Rodkey, Jason Vrabel, Nic Eaton, Gwendolyn Kiste, Jason Peck, David Joez Villaverde, Jessica Simms, the writers and readers of the Rahnd Table and Hour After Happy Hour workshops, Dasha Borisenko-Orlowski for help with Russian idioms and folklore, César Maxit and Priscila Castaño for fixing my terrible Argentine Spanish, Stephen Scheboth for Photoshop wizardry, my partner Hillary Lazar for all of her support, and Nathan Kukulski and Six Gallery Press for believing in this book and launching it into the world.

"What Is There to Say" previously appeared in *F(r)iction* Issue 8.

"Stop Me If You've Heard This One Before" previously appeared in *Versal* Issue 9.

"White People" previously appeared in *The After Happy Hour Review* Issue 3.

"Our Hero" previously appeared in *Flapperhouse* XX.

"The Collector" previously appeared in *Sanitarium* Issue 46.

"The Number 9 Train" previously appeared in *Paragraphiti*.

"Robot on a Park Bench" previously appeared in *Delmarva Review* Vol. 7.

"Stan's Taxidermy Express" previously appeared as "Skins" in *Burrow Press Review*.

"The Lone Hero and the Self-Made Man" previously appeared in *Pif Magazine*.

"Lesser Demons" previously appeared as "What They Know" in *Cheat River Review*.

Brandon Getz earned an MFA in fiction writing from Eastern Washington University. His work has appeared in *F(r)iction*, *Versal*, *Flapperhouse*, and elsewhere. His debut novel, *Lars Breaxface: Werewolf in Space*—an irreverent sci-fi monster adventure—was released in October 2019 from Spaceboy Books. He lives in Pittsburgh, PA.